'Daniel?'

He turned his head to look at her. 'Can we do that, Sophie? Can we put everything behind us? You were sleeping with my brother at the same time you were sleeping with me. Did you tell Michael you loved him as well, or did you save that particular honour for me?'

Sophie shut her eyes at the accusation in his voice. How could he think that of her? The denial came to her lips, but she quashed the impulse to clear her character. There had been four years of lies trapping her in a web that just got stickier.

A&E DRAMA

Blood pressure is high and pulses are racing in these
fast-paced dramatic stories from Mills & Boon®
Medical Romance™. They'll move a mountain
to save a life in an emergency, be they the crash team,
emergency doctors, or paramedics. There are lots of
critical engagements amongst the high tensions
and emotional passions in these exciting stories
of lives and loves at risk!

Recent titles by the same author:

EARTHQUAKE BABY
THE MIDWIFE'S MIRACLE BABY

THE NURSE'S SECRET SON

BY
AMY ANDREWS

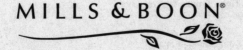

This book is dedicated to all my colleagues in the Samford First
Responder Group, and to Mick at Grovely for his mentoring

First published in Great Britain 2006
Harlequin Mills & Boon Limited,
Eton House, 18-24 Paradise Road, Richmond, Surrey TW9 1SR

© Amy Andrews 2006

ISBN 0 263 84707 1

Set in Times Roman 10½ on 13 pt.
03-0106-48673

Printed and bound in Spain
by Litografia Rosés, S.A., Barcelona

PROLOGUE

DANIEL MONDAY frowned as the ringing of the bedside phone interrupted his familiar dream. The woman beside him protested sleepily as he rose on one elbow and plucked it off the cradle. The red digital figures of the clock told him it was three a.m.

'Yes?' He heard the tension that had crawled across his shoulders reflected in his voice. His blue eyes mirrored his concern. No one rang at three in the morning with good news.

There was silence on the other end and Daniel felt his ire rise at being woken in the middle of the night by a prank call. 'Is anyone there?' he asked curtly.

'Daniel…it's me…Sophie.'

Daniel felt the tension in his shoulder muscles intensify as the woman from his dream spoke into his ear. He rose slowly from the bed, careful not to disturb the leggy redhead, and wandered into the lounge room. What did Sophie want?

'It's three in the morning, Sophie—what do you want?' He knew he sounded gruff but it was late and…he didn't need this. He didn't need a late-night trans-Pacific phone call undoing all the emotional distance he'd achieved. Hell!

He'd moved to New York. Started a new life. He didn't need her to unsettle his equilibrium again.

'It's John…'

Daniel heard the catch in her voice and felt his heart start to pound. Something really bad must have occurred for her to be ringing at this time. 'Grandfather? What's happened to G.?'

'He's had a CVA.'

'A stroke?' The pounding was almost deafening now as he tried to recall everything he knew about cerebral-vascular accidents. 'But he's so fit and healthy.'

'He's eighty-four, Daniel.'

'Which side is it? Is it bad?' His medical training had taken over now, the questions he needed to ask to assess his grandfather's condition forming clearly in his mind.

'It was a right CVA. He's totally paralysed down his left side. He's stable but the next 48 hours will be critical. His neurologist won't know the full residual effect until the swelling dissipates. He's asking for you, Daniel. He's very distressed.'

Daniel clutched the phone, forcing himself to concentrate on the information and not to dwell on the emotion in Sophie's voice. 'So his speech is OK?' asked Daniel, still in clinical mode. That was positive.

'It's not great. He's very difficult to understand.'

Daniel closed his eyes and imagined his strong, intelligent grandfather lying helpless in a hospital bed. How he would hate it.

'Will you come home, Daniel?'

'As soon as I can arrange it. I'll get on to the airline now. It'll still probably be the day after tomorrow with the time difference.'

A silence fell over the line. Was she thinking the same as him? Did John have that long? Would he get there in time?

'Thank you, Daniel. If anyone can get him through this, you can.'

He nodded, knowing she was right. He had always known he was the apple of his grandfather's eye. Not seeing John was probably one of the hardest parts of his self-imposed exile.

'Are you OK?' Daniel said the words before he could stop himself. Before he could remind himself that he was still angry with her. But her voice sounded shaky and he knew how close she also was to John.

'Sure,' she said, and he could hear her sniff. 'It's been a shock and it's awful to see him so…still. Max is very upset. He found John on the floor and he's too young to understand. He keeps asking for his G.G.'

Daniel felt his heart go out to his nephew. The poor little guy. He'd already lost his father. It must have been awful for a three-year-old to discover his normally active great-grandfather sprawled helplessly on the floor. Even from the other side of the world Daniel knew that Max and John had a very close relationship.

'Where is the little tyke?'

'He's at Arabella with Sally.'

Thank goodness for Sally. Daniel wondered with all the things that had happened in the last four years how the Monday family would have coped without their unflappable housekeeper.

'Have you rung the rest of the family?'

'Your parents are flying back from Europe as we speak.'

'Good. OK,' said Daniel. It was time for him to ring off

but now her voice was in his ear again he found it an almost impossible task. Her voice stirred memories. 'I should go—get things organised.'

Sophie walked silently into Max's bedroom and watched him sleep. She'd been by John's side all day and she had missed her little man. She hoped to take him to see his G.G. as soon as possible to allay Max's fears and she was certain it would also be a real boost for John.

Not as much as Daniel's arrival would be, however. The prodigal grandson would be greeted with much joy even if John Monday would be physically incapable of expressing it. She could feel her own anticipation building and had to remind herself how much Daniel had hurt her. How the hurt and anger had erected a wall of bitterness between them.

Sophie stroked her finger down Max's cute button nose and watched his chest rise and fall.

'Daddy's coming home, my baby,' she whispered. 'Daddy's coming home.'

CHAPTER ONE

SOPHIE buckled a sleeping Max into his car seat and shut the door. She looked up at the leaden sky and thought, How appropriate! Still, at least the inclement weather had held off until now.

Getting away had been just what she had needed. The stress of the last few days had taken its toll. Watching John slip in and out of consciousness had been very worrying.

Worse was witnessing his frustration at being unable to communicate properly during his waking moments. For such an articulate man, being robbed of his speech had been the worst insult.

She had gratefully accepted her mother-in-law's invitation to get away to the holiday house for a couple of days. John's condition had stabilised and now they were back from Europe she had been relieved from her bedside vigil.

Max had needed this time away, too. He had been clingy and upset since his great-grandfather had been taken ill, and dividing herself between her son and John had been exhausting. He had needed reassurance and she had been able to give him that these last two days when it had been just the two of them.

And then there was Daniel. His plane had touched down yesterday and Sophie had felt too wrung out and emotionally shot to deal with all their personal baggage as well. She was going to have to face him soon but the lingering memory of the last time they'd seen each other and the shame and loathing it always aroused didn't make her in any hurry.

She threw her small bag into the boot of her car and let her hand linger on the bright yellow paintwork as she shut it. She loved her Beetle. Michael had bought it for her for their first anniversary.

Michael. Sophie felt the familiar rush of mixed feelings rise like a tidal wave inside. The acute sense of loss and grief had started to dissipate but it occasionally still threatened to overwhelm her. She made a conscious effort to concentrate on the pink flower on her dashboard as she buckled up. She felt the wave ebb and sighed gratefully.

Not for the first time, she wondered how different her life would be now if Michael hadn't become a paraplegic and she had been emotionally free to marry the man she had truly loved, instead of settling for his brother. Guilt and pity and platonic love and long-standing friendship had been a strong catalyst and she'd been…happy.

But with Daniel back on the scene, he would be a constant reminder of a tumultuous part of her life. There was bound to be a resurfacing of all the hurt and guilt and anger that had made their previously carefree relationship a minefield of recriminations.

She reversed out of the garage into the steadily falling rain and thanked the gods for the divine weather of the last two days. Max loved visiting the holiday home. But, then, so did she. Set high on a hill overlooking the beckoning Pacific, a short drive from Noosa, who wouldn't?

They'd had a ball, building sandcastles on the beach and swimming in the luxurious pool. She had seen the worry in her son's eyes ease and the incessant questions about John slow to a trickle as he'd realised that his world hadn't changed too much.

Of course, visiting his great-grandfather briefly at St Jude's on their way to the coast had been very beneficial in this process. Max had been able to see for himself that John wasn't dead, that they hadn't been lying to him.

Sophie's eyes had welled with tears as Max had planted a kiss on John's cheek and said, 'I wuv you, G.G.' She'd noticed tears shining in the old man's eyes, too and she had swallowed hard and looked away, battling to regain her composure. John didn't need his support structures falling apart. That's why this break had been so important. To re-group. But now it was time to go home.

She looked down at the sleeveless white vest she had thrown on after whipping off her bikini top down on the secluded beach. Her denim cut-off shorts were damp from having climbed into them while she'd still been wet from the ocean. There wouldn't be much call for her to wear this outfit for a while.

It was amazing that in just two days the sun had coaxed her slender arms and long legs to turn a lovely shade of caramel brown. It emphasised her dark blue eyes and the natural caramel streaks in her blonde hair.

The car crawled down the winding dirt driveway as the rain and the encroaching dusk reduced visibility. The surface was a little slippery too and Sophie was grateful when the road flattened out. She rounded the last bend before the gate and slammed her brakes on hard, sliding to a halt.

A ute blocked the road at a crazy angle, the driver's door wide open. Sophie recognised the vehicle immediately as belonging to Charlie, Sally's husband. The couple had kept house for the Mondays for two decades and Charlie had been responsible for the magnificence of the gardens, both here and at Arabella, the Monday family mansion in Brisbane.

Sophie was momentarily puzzled. The car didn't appear to be damaged so an accident seemed unlikely despite the atrocious driving conditions. A breakdown maybe? But…where was Charlie?

And then she saw him through the gloom. A figure lying on the ground, face up, near a rear wheel.

'Oh, my God,' she whispered as her nursing instincts urged her body to action. She glanced at Max, who was still sleeping soundly. She grabbed her mobile, praying for decent coverage, and flung her door open. She went directly to her boot, pulled out the first-aid kit and bolted to Charlie's side.

The rain drenched her in seconds. It didn't matter. Only Charlie mattered.

'Charlie! Charlie!' she called, as she knelt in the mud and shook him. She ignored the tiny hard rocks that dug into her knees like needles. She grabbed the torch from the first-aid kit and shone it in his face.

'Damn,' she swore, as the gravity of the situation became apparent.

It was obvious Charlie had had a massive allergic reaction to something. He'd seemed perfectly fine ten minutes ago when she had waved him good bye, so it had to be anaphylactic shock. Bees. She remembered he was allergic to bees.

His face had swollen dramatically, his eyes puffed to the point of being shut. His face looked grotesque. Ogre-like. The skin was shiny, stretched beyond its normal elasticity. He was flushed and had huge red welts covering his body.

'Charlie!' she called again as she ground her fist into his sternum, hoping to gain some response. He was unconscious. She felt his carotid pulse and was relieved to find he had one but unsurprised by its weak, erratic beat. He was fading. Fast.

Sophie heard the distinctive raspy noise of obstructed breathing. She prised his mouth open and inspected his large swollen tongue. Soon it would totally occlude his airway.

She dialled triple zero. 'Yes, I need an ambulance,' she said, raising her voice to be heard above the rain which was bucketing down, plastering her caramel blonde hair to her head and her clothes to her body.

Sophie gave the details to the ambulance call-taker while monitoring Charlie's pulse and breathing. As she talked she was thinking. Adrenaline. Didn't Charlie usually carry the lifesaving drug?

She looked around and noticed for the first time the contents of a small toiletry bag strewn on the ground around Charlie. Had he been trying to get to his vital injection when he'd lost consciousness?

She nearly cheered out loud as she shone the torch on the Adrenipen, which had rolled out of Charlie's reach just under the car. It was aptly named. Looking like an ordinary pen, inside the barrel a cartridge of adrenaline replaced ink. The nib was a fine needle. It was a simple single-use unit that anyone could be taught to use, even a child.

She reached over him, extracting it and checking it was ready to go. Still talking to the ambulance call-taker, Sophie plunged the pen into his upper arm muscle and depressed the button on the end to deliver the entire contents into his system.

Sophie was relieved to feel Charlie's pulse strengthen but dismayed to hear that the inclement weather had stretched the ambulance service to its limit. Paramedics were being despatched but due to their relative isolation the ETA was twenty minutes. Charlie didn't have twenty minutes.

Just then a car engine and a set of headlights intruded into her frantic thoughts. Sophie could have cried she was that grateful. She watched the man get out of his car, the heavy rain obscuring his face, and waved him over.

'What happened?' he asked, kneeling beside her.

Sophie turned to explain and stopped, the words dying on her lips. 'Daniel?' she shouted above the rain, drips of water hanging off her sodden fringe.

'Sophie?'

They stared at each other. Years of love, hate, anger, friendship, guilt, bitterness and…yearning filled the space between them.

'What are you doing here?' she asked. 'I thought you were with John? He's OK, isn't he?' Alarm raised her voice even further. He should be with John.

'He's fine. I came to talk to you. But,' he said, looking down at Charlie, 'it can wait.' They clearly had an emergency on their hands. He had to concentrate on that. 'What's happened to Charlie?'

Sophie made room for Daniel to assess their patient. Relief to have an intensive care paramedic by her side flooded through her. She could put all the other issues aside if he could. Charlie would die unless they did something.

'Allergic reaction?'

'I'm assuming it was a bee,' she confirmed.

'How long ago?'

'Not sure. He was ten minutes ahead of me and I've been here close to ten minutes. Depends when he was bitten. Twenty minutes tops.'

'He's lucky you came along.'

'He's had a hit of adrenaline but he needs more.'

'And some hydrocortisone and an antihistamine,' he agreed, switching to clinical mode.

'Oxygen would be handy, too.'

'He's barely breathing and cyanosed,' Daniel observed as Sophie noticed the blue tinge starting to stain Charlie's lips.

'Ambulance is still fifteen minutes away,' she said, using the torchlight to consult her watch.

Daniel had never wanted his trauma kit more. Here, on the roadside in the pouring rain with no equipment, no drugs and no shelter, there didn't seem much hope. But he did have a fully qualified emergency nurse by his side, which was an asset he knew you couldn't put a value on.

He had to think of her like that. As a nurse. An asset. A card he held to help save Charlie's life. Because if he thought of her as Sophie, his Sophie—the girl he'd taught to climb trees, to ride a bike and where to kick a guy who wouldn't take no for an answer—he would be of no use to Charlie.

He shook his head, flinging water droplets into the air that joined the others belting down from the sky. Damn the rain! Damn the bad visibility. And damn Sophie. Damn her for still being as beautiful as she was in his dreams.

Daniel put his head right down to Charlie's mouth, concerned that the laboured breathing they were both so attuned to, despite the noise of the rain, had stopped. It had!

'He's stopped breathing.'

'Damn it, Charlie! Don't do this to us.' Sophie gave their patient a shake. She pulled a resus mask out of her first-aid kit and fitted it over Charlie's nose and mouth.

'I don't think you're going to be able to oxygenate him that way,' said Daniel, adjusting Charlie's neck for her so she could hold the mask in place properly. 'His airway is totally obstructed.'

'I know,' she admitted, 'but maybe we can get some through. You watch his chest.'

Sophie blew into the port at the top of the rubber mask that formed a mouthpiece. She repeated the exercise a few times.

'No chest movement,' said Daniel. 'It's no good, we'll have to trachy him.'

'What?' Sophie stared at him like he'd just suggested they put a gun to Charlie's head and shoot him. 'Are you crazy? How? What with? We can hardly see each other, let alone perform an operation on his neck!'

'It's the only way, Sophie, trust me,' he said, running to his car.

Twice. Since he'd left for New York she'd seen him twice. And now he was asking her to trust him. Sophie frantically attempted to push some more air into Charlie's lungs but his chest remained deathly still. The strange thing was, she did trust him. Before this rocky patch she had trusted him implicitly and, despite everything, here in the pouring rain, trying to save Charlie's life, she still did.

Daniel hurried back with a pocket-knife and a black

ballpoint pen with the ink cartridge removed. It was now just a hollow plastic tube.

She stared at him through the lashing rain and swallowed hard. He was really going to do this. Sophie had seen many tracheostomies being performed, both in the controlled environment of an operating theatre and in critical situations in the accident and emergency department. But in the field?

She didn't want to think about it. Only she had to because every second Charlie went without oxygen took him a step closer to irreversible brain damage, cardiac arrest and death.

'Please, tell me you've done this before.' She placed a stilling hand on his as he quickly prepared his equipment.

'I've done this before.'

She smiled at him then. Water rivulets ran over her lips, moistening them, and a sudden rush of desire kicked him hard in the solar plexus.

'Come on, then, Daniel.' She smiled, his confidence infectious. 'Time is brain cells.'

He instructed Sophie to extend Charlie's neck. She did so with one hand and held the torch with the other. Daniel noted her professional hold, knowing that she was monitoring Charlie's carotid pulse, as well as giving Charlie good jaw support to optimise his airway. Once again he found himself grateful to have such a skilled assistant.

Daniel ran an index finger down the hard ridges of cartilage that formed Charlie's trachea until he identified the Adam's apple, or thyroid cartilage. He kept his finger there and slid his middle finger lower until he found the cricoid cartilage. The indentation between the two was where he would make his incision.

He drew a steadying breath and sensed Sophie tense as he positioned the knife. Daniel made a small horizontal incision in the cricothyroid membrane and felt the give as the knife entered the trachea. There was surprisingly little blood.

He placed his finger inside the slit to open it slightly to allow passage of the hollow pen. He pushed the plastic tube into the stoma he had created—it was a snug fit. He blew some deep breaths into the artificial airway and only acknowledged his thundering heart when he saw Charlie's chest rise and fall again.

'You did it, Daniel! You did it!' It had seemed like an age to Sophie yet in reality the procedure had taken about twenty seconds.

Daniel smiled around the pen keeping his eyes down so he couldn't see her brilliant smile, her triumphant face or the way the rivulets of rain ran down her neck and chest into her soaked and clinging shirt. Seeing that was not good for his concentration.

Sophie's celebrations were short-lived, however, as she felt Charlie's pulse slow, become irregular and then stop.

'Lost his pulse.' Sophie tried to keep the alarm out of her voice. She was a professional. She knew what to do. But this wasn't some anonymous patient. This was Charlie.

'You do chest compressions,' Daniel said between breaths.

Sophie shifted position and started compressing Charlie's sternum with her interlocked hands. They couldn't lose him after all this.

They fell into a routine, he delivered one breath for every five of her compressions. Daniel couldn't help himself. He looked out the corner of his eye as her rhythmic shoulder movements caused her breasts to bounce. The rain ran down her bare arms and plastered the fabric of her shirt to her breasts, moulding them, the nipples on show to the world. He tried not to think of the hours he had spent touching them and how she used to beg him to never stop.

Sophie glanced at him and caught him staring. There was an intensity in his incredibly blue eyes that was compelling. Was he…he appeared to be…staring at her breasts? She looked down at them as she kept up the rhythm on Charlie's chest.

She almost gasped. Her top was clinging to her braless form, leaving nothing to the imagination. She was mortified. She may as well have PLEASE OGLE MY BOOBS tattooed on her forehead! She felt her cheeks grow warm and looked away.

A rush of memories assailed her. It was hard to believe from their current strained relationship that there had been a time when they hadn't been able to get enough of each other. When making love had been a desperate, urgent need that they had slaked as often as they could.

A siren blaring in the distance pulled her out of the past and an ambulance pulled up a minute later. Three paramedics dressed in rain gear hurried to them.

'Hi, Jane Carter, I'm a paramedic. What's happened here?' Her friendly voice was a welcome distraction and Sophie noted the stripes on her shoulder indicating Jane's intensive care status.

'Sophie, swap with me,' said Daniel, shuffling along so they could change positions. Daniel took over chest compressions, allowing him to talk.

'Daniel Monday, off-duty paramedic. Anaphylactic

shock following an assumed beesting. Adrenaline administered via Adrenipen. I performed a tracheostomy due to complete upper airway obstruction from the tongue—'

'You did?'

Sophie smiled at the incredulous note in Jane's voice. 'Don't worry, Jane, he's an IC para, like you,' she said, lifting her mouth briefly from the plastic tube and then returning to her task.

'He needs a trachy tube, IV access, fluids, more adrenaline, as well as some hydrocortisone and Phenergan.'

'You trachied him,' Jane repeated, her stunned expression still firmly in place. 'Good call.'

The paramedics sprang into action, relieving Sophie of her job. She rose slowly, the skin on her knees abraded by the constant needling of tiny sharp rocks. They were muddy and bloodied.

'Get in the back of the ambulance,' one of the paramedics offered. 'There's blankets to dry off and keep warm.'

Sophie checked on a still sleeping Max first and then gratefully sought the shelter offered. The flashing red emergency lights still active on its roof gave the ambulance a welcoming glow. It beckoned her, all dry and warm.

She wrapped a white cellular blanket around herself and watched as Daniel and the three paramedics continued to work on Charlie.

Daniel placed a proper tube into the hole he had created in Charlie's trachea and they attached a bag to the end to administer lungfuls of one hundred per cent oxygen.

'How long has he been down?' Jane asked.

'He went into cardiac arrest only a couple minutes before you got here. He stopped breathing about ten minutes ago but his ventilation has probably been severely compromised for about twenty minutes.' Daniel's reply was methodical. Concise.

Sophie was relieved to see a cardiac rhythm come back quickly after adrenaline was administered down the trachy tube and directly into the lungs. She started to feel a spark of hope.

Twenty minutes later Charlie was as stabilised as they could get him in the rain on a roadside. They loaded him into the ambulance and Daniel and Sophie watched its flashing red lights until it disappeared from sight.

They stood in silence for a moment as the rain finally eased to a light shower.

'Well, this'll be something I won't forget in a hurry,' said Daniel.

'You can say that again,' she said, and gave a half-laugh. She turned to face him. Now the emergency was over she didn't know what to say. It had been two years since she'd last seen him and the terrible things they had both said still seemed so fresh they could have spoken them yesterday.

'Why don't we go back to the house? I think we need to talk.'

'No.' She shook her head. 'I need to get back. Sally needs to know about Charlie. I don't want her to hear it over the phone and I have Max in the car.'

He shot her a measured look. 'How is my little nephew? Mum said you took him to see G.'

'Yes, he's much happier now.'

The rain continued to sprinkle down around them as another silence fell between them.

'We need to talk, Sophie. We're going to be seeing a lot of each other. G. needs support and harmony, not—'

'I assume you're staying at Arabella?' she asked, interrupting him as she thought quickly ahead. She didn't want to have this conversation with him now. In the growing darkness, in the rain, in soaked clothes, with Max asleep in the car and with Charlie's emergency and John's stroke weighing heavily on her mind. She was a little too overwhelmed to think straight. If this conversation turned out like their last then she'd need to have her wits about her.

'In my old room,' he said, a small smile on his lips.

'OK,' she said, shrugging the heavy, sodden blanket from her shoulders and opening her car door. She needed action. Anything to take her mind off the things they had done in that room. 'We can talk tomorrow.'

Sophie seated her drenched body in her beautiful car pleased to see that Max had slept his way through the whole incident. She started the car and realised she hadn't even thanked Daniel. They may have had their problems but she knew one thing for sure—Charlie would be dead right now if he hadn't come along when he had. She pressed the button for the electric window and it slid down with a soft whirr.

'Thanks,' she said, hating the husky note that had crept into her voice.

He nodded at her wordlessly and she drove away carefully. Sophie watched the unmoving form of Daniel in her rear-view mirror until the rain and night totally obscured him. Her arms and legs started to shake as reaction from the events of the night sank in. She shivered and turned the heater on high.

So, Daniel had come back. She had asked and he had come. And he was living at Arabella. Well, it was his home after all. Much more his than hers. She shifted uncomfortably in her seat, the wet denim of her shorts chafing her thighs. Could they live under the same roof?

She pushed her disturbing thoughts aside and switched on the radio. The DJ announced a mushy love song in a chirpy voice and she quickly changed channels. A hard rock song blared out and she turned up the volume. Anything to stop herself thinking about Daniel.

Daniel stayed rooted to the spot for who knew how long. Long after her car lights disappeared. Long after the rain finally stopped.

She was still exactly the same.

Still the same girl who had shadowed him constantly when she'd been five and he eleven.

Still the beautiful teenager who had begged him for her first kiss when she'd been sixteen.

Still the desirable woman who had given him the gift of her virginity and had told him she loved him.

Still the woman who had married his brother instead.

Still the woman who had slept with him mere hours after they had laid his brother, cold and dead, in his grave.

How could she have done that? How could he?

CHAPTER TWO

DANIEL tracked Sophie down the next afternoon on his return from the beach house. They had to have that talk. The way things had been left between them could make living under the same roof very difficult. There were things that needed to be said.

After enquiring about Charlie and finding out he'd already been transferred from ICU to a ward, Daniel came straight to the point. 'About what happened after Michael's funeral, the things we said.'

Sophie felt nauseous, thinking about it. It hadn't been the highlight of their tangled relationship.

'It was something that shouldn't have happened,' Daniel said.

'Yes, thank you, I got that.'

'Look. I'm sorry. I shouldn't have said the things that I did. I was just a little…shocked at our—my—behaviour and I handled it very badly.'

Sophie almost laughed out loud at the extent of his understatement.

'I'd just buried my brother, Sophie. I wasn't thinking straight.'

OK. That was it. He wasn't going to pull the grieving brother card. 'Well, gee, Daniel, I'd just buried my husband but I didn't accuse you of being some kind of Jezebel or whatever the hell the male equivalent is.'

'I know. I know. I'm sorry. I really am.'

'It takes two to tango, Daniel. I didn't notice you trying to put the brakes on.' Sophie was surprised at how raw her hurt still was.

He shut his eyes and tried to erase the images that sprang into his head. He didn't want to go over that night blow by blow—he just wanted to clear the air over it. Obviously she was still hurting from their angry exchange of words.

'Look. All I wanted to say was I'm sorry that it happened and sorry for what I said. We both have to live under this roof and I'd like to be able to get past what happened.'

And if they did? Weren't there still a thousand other things between them that were also hard to get past? 'And what about all the other stuff, Daniel?'

'Well, I don't know about you but I'm over all the other stuff. I thought you would be by now, too.' It was important that she knew that up front. He was over her.

Sophie saw red. What exactly was he trying to imply? 'I am one hundred per cent over you, Daniel Monday. As far as I'm concerned, you and I never existed.'

Good, he thought, they understood each other. He didn't need any rekindling of old flames. Michael might be dead but his obligations to his brother hadn't died with him. He owed his brother and Sophie belonged to Michael. Period.

And that was the last conversation they had for a while. The entire family devoted their time to keeping John company at St Jude's and Daniel and Sophie fell into a pattern.

For the three weeks John was hospitalised they rarely saw each other. Sophie took some leave, spending the days with Max and then heading off to St Jude's at night, while Max was sleeping, to read to John.

Daniel spent the mornings with John and spent the afternoons making the necessary arrangements to pack up his New York life and find a job. He wanted to be around for John. Seeing his strong, able-bodied grandfather so dependent had been a wake-up call. John wasn't a young man and Daniel wanted to be there for his grandfather's twilight years, just as his grandfather had always been there for him.

Once John's cerebral oedema had settled he improved quite quickly, regaining a good portion of the function he had lost. His gag and swallow reflex had returned to almost normal by the end of the first week and his speech improved dramatically with just occasional slurring of some words. That had been a great relief to everyone as John's frustration was making him very cranky.

The left-sided paralysis had lessened but there was still a significant residual deficit on that side and he was going to need intense physiotherapy to regain the power and use of his limbs. Mobilisation was limited, with John relying heavily on a wheelchair.

But nothing on earth was going to keep John in St Jude's a moment longer than he needed to be. Not the private room, not the attentions of the top neurologist or the very best of everything St Jude's could lay on. He had spent too many years walking its corridors as an eminent professor of microbiology to suddenly be in a position where he felt vulnerable and powerless.

And the stroke certainly hadn't affected his obstinate

streak. He was eighty-four and had suffered a huge cerebral insult, but he remained sharp as a tack and determined to make a full recovery. At home. At Arabella. Surrounded by his family and everything dear and familiar to him.

Luckily Arabella was already equipped for a wheelchair. It had been fully converted for Michael—ramps, rails and even a lift to the upper storey had been installed. Hallways and doorways had been widened where necessary. All the conversions money could buy had been put in place. Little had they known that not one but two Mondays would benefit from the changes.

The family had arranged the best care in Brisbane. A private physiotherapist and nurse had been arranged to come in on a daily basis. They'd also consulted other allied health fields and a private occupational and speech therapist would also be involved in John's care.

When the big homecoming day finally arrived, Sophie was relieved as splitting herself in two was quite exhausting. She and Max had shifted from their wing to make way for John as these rooms were the most wheelchair friendly. Michael, Sophie and Max had lived in them as a family so they were decked out with every device imaginable to make living in a wheelchair as easy as possible.

They moved into the guest wing with much excitement on Max's side. Sophie not as much. She knew that it was the most sensible thing for John but she had a sense that things were changing in her life that were beyond her control. Daniel's presence only intensified this feeling.

Her living space hadn't changed in four years and she'd never realised what a security blanket it was. The love and the laughter the three of them had shared in these rooms was difficult to let go of. It was so silly. She was just moving down the corridor and yet it seemed like a whole new world.

In fact, as she had shifted their belongings she had even contemplated moving out altogether. Maybe it was time to make a clean break? Living with Daniel was going to be awkward and even though Sophie looked upon Arabella as her home she had no real claim on it and even less now that Michael was dead.

Wendy and Edward, Michael and Daniel's parents, were horrified when she had broached the subject at dinner one night.

'Goodness, Sophie! What do you mean, move out? That's the most ridiculous thing I've ever heard!' Edward had said, dropping his fork on his plate with a clatter.

'It's getting a little crowded here now. I don't want you to feel you have to keep providing a place for me to live. You've been very generous, opening up your home to me.'

'Yours as well, Sophie,' Wendy interrupted, tears shining in her eyes. 'It's high time you started thinking of Arabella as your home, too. For goodness' sake, you've been coming here every school holiday since you were five and lived here permanently since your uni years. Max hasn't known another home. No.' She shook her head. 'We won't hear of it. Arabella is as much your home as ours.'

Sophie had felt warmed by her mother-in-law's affirmation but as she and Max sat waiting for John to arrive she also remembered Daniel's silence during that conversation.

This house held plenty of their history, too. So many happy times. She smiled as she thought about them now. Times when Michael and Sophie had followed the older Daniel around like puppies.

Times the three of them had spent up the mulberry tree, eating handfuls of the sweet berries until their clothes and fingers and lips had been stained dark purple. Times when they'd splashed in the pool. Times when they'd skipped stones across the surface of the Brisbane river that lapped at the edges of Arabella's extensive grounds.

And the time when, long after he'd moved out, she and Daniel had realised they loved each other and had spent weeks sneaking around, meeting secretly to kiss and touch and whisper sweet nothings.

They had kept their new relationship quiet, wanting to savour it by themselves for a while. Carry on without the fuss and attention that they'd known would be made of it. Kissing in the gardens, in the pool, in the bathrooms and in his bedroom. Finally making love on his old bed and knowing they wanted to be together for ever.

And as Max jumped off the bed at the sound of the car in the driveway and she saw Daniel in the driver's seat, she remembered the bad times as well.

Learning about the accident and that Michael, her best friend, was going to be a paraplegic for the rest of his life, discovering she was pregnant and then Daniel's rejection.

'I don't love you. I never loved you. I just said that so you'd have sex with me.'

She remembered how harsh his voice had been and his sneer and her total devastation as her world, already crumbling from Michael's tragedy, had crashed in a heap around her. How the news about their baby had died on her lips and she'd realised she couldn't tell him. Not after he had said such an awful thing.

'Come on, Mummy,' said Max, jumping up and down on the bed excitedly. 'G.G.'s home!'

He grabbed her hand and heaved with all his three-year-old might to pull her off the bed. She smiled at her snowy-haired son and felt tears sting her eyes. Oh, to be so carefree!

'Mummy's coming,' she sniffed, and swallowed the hurt along with her tears.

A week later Sophie walked into the entrance to St Jude's Hospital and made her way through the sliding doors of the ground-floor accident and emergency department. She greeted the three other RNs who were waiting for handover from Georgina, the department's nurse manager.

She sighed contentedly—it was great to be back at work. It would give her a break from the constant state of wariness she now lived in. Running into Daniel was becoming a more frequent occurrence now that John was home, and she was finding the situation increasingly difficult.

Her anger with him warred with rekindled memories and she found herself increasingly just wanting to shout at him. For his rejection, for his distance and for seducing her at an emotionally crippling time of her life and then treating her like…Eve who had tempted him with the forbidden apple. Oh, yeah. She was definitely mad at him.

'In cubicle one,' Georgina interrupted Sophie's turbulent thoughts, 'we have a twenty-three-year-old female with abdominal pain. We're waiting on blood and urine results. She's had fifty of pethidine and her pain has settled.'

'Any bleeding?' asked Sophie, snapping into her clinical role.

'No. Not gynae. Preg. test is negative.'

'Cube two is a sixty-year-old female with a chest infection. X-ray shows left lobe consolidation.'

'Antibiotics?' asked Richard.

'Stat dose of penicillin. Sputum samples have been sent.'

'Let me guess. We're waiting on a ward bed,' said Richard, his voice heavy with derision. Bed shortages were always a problem.

Georgina nodded and continued. 'Cubes three and four are empty. Cube five is a forty-two-year-old male who sliced open his left lower arm on some kind of industrial saw thing at work a couple of hours ago.'

'Ugh! Did he lose much blood?' asked Leah.

'Estimated loss of approximately two hundred mils. He's lucky there's been no damage to any major vessels, tendons or nerves. He's scheduled for suturing as soon as Todd's ready.'

Oh, goody! Todd was on—they were definitely going to have a great night. Dr Todd Hutchinson was one of the department's registrars. He was nearly at the end of his six-month rotation. He had blond curly hair and looked about nineteen instead of thirty. His youthful looks gave him an air of innocence despite his dreadful habit of practical joking. He was a laugh a minute. And a dreadful flirt. Sophie really enjoyed working with him.

'Cubes six, seven and eight are also vacant. The six beds in Short Stay, however, are packed to the roof. There's been a vomiting and diarrhoea bug going around since the Ekka started. Everyone's on IV fluids and anti-emetics.'

They all had a chuckle. Every year the same thing happened. The yearly agricultural exhibition came to town with its sideshow alley and carnival atmosphere, and everyone in Brisbane came down with whatever the prevalent illness happened to be at the time. Last year it had been flu, the year before conjunctivitis. When hundreds of thousands of people mingled, there was bound to be some germ swapping!

'No one's in Resus and there's nothing around the ridges that I know of. You should have a quiet shift.'

Leah looked at Sophie then at her boss and said, 'Thanks, George! Give us the kiss of death, why don't you? When the bus-crash victims start rolling though the door you'll be the first one we call.' They all laughed.

As Sophie had seniority it was her job to allocate the late-shift staff to the areas they would work in until they knocked off at eleven p.m.

'Richard, can I give you Short Stay?' She batted her eyelids dramatically and smiled her sweetest pleading smile. Eight hours with vomit bowls and bedpans was a very long time!

'But, of course, Sophie, my dear. I love vomit. I live for vomit. Vomit is my best friend.' He rolled his eyes.

'You're a darling.' She giggled. They watched as he stuffed his pockets full of disposable gloves until they were bulging then donned special splash goggles and a plastic apron. He looked ready to do battle.

'Karen, you can do Triage.'

'Are you sure?' Karen's smile was hesitant. She was a new graduate who had only been in the department for a few months and this would be her first time solo at the triage desk.

'Positive. You'll be great. You're a natural.' Sophie shot

her a reassuring smile and watched as Karen blushed. 'Just come and ask if you're not sure about anything.'

They watched as Karen headed to the desk, a spring in her step. 'OK, babe,' she said to Leah. 'You and me got the cubes. Reckon we can handle it?'

'With our eyes shut.'

Sophie grinned at her friend. She felt the stress of the last month lift a little. She loved her work here at St Jude's. Being an emergency nurse had always been her goal and she had come straight to the department from her training five years before.

They had been tremendous during her times of need. Like Michael's accident and the numerous times she had needed leave at a moment's notice in the beginning to grapple with some new crisis due to his paralysis. And then maternity leave and the whole awful time surrounding Michael's sudden death two years later. She couldn't have asked for a more supportive workplace.

She only worked part time these days, mainly night duty with the occasional late shift. She didn't want to be disruptive to Max and his routine and found these shifts suited best.

Michael had been house-husband when he'd been alive and she had worked full time. His male pride had occasionally been pricked but he had thrived in his role and Sophie had loved how close he and Max had been. Especially when Michael had always known Max was not his son but had loved him like his own regardless.

'Sophie, don't forget you're rostered on at the city station for your yearly ambulance ride-along on Saturday night,' Georgina reminded her as she walked past on her way out.

Damn it! She had forgotten, with everything that had happened recently.

'Sophie!'

A low whistle from behind had her turning around. 'Hey, Todd.' She grinned.

'Look at you.' He laughed. 'You look great. Fantastic tan,' he said, stroking his hand lightly down her sun-kissed arm. 'How's the professor?'

'In much better humour now he's at home,' she said.

Their conversation was interrupted by a commotion coming from the triage desk. Leah, Richard, Todd and herself went to investigate.

An elderly woman—Sophie thought she might be in her eighties—was babbling away in a foreign language and gesticulating wildly at Karen. The young nurse looked bewildered, getting a word in when she could. Another woman—about her own age, Sophie thought—was adding her voice to the hubbub, trying to calm the older woman.

Sophie dug Richard in the ribs. His smooth charm had calmed many an agitated patient. He moved forward into the fray, ever-present vomit bowl in hand.

He stood beside the elderly lady and she turned to glare at him. Then she said something that sounded suspiciously like an insult and promptly threw up into Richard's bowl.

A few seconds of stunned silence followed.

'Well done, good catch, Richard,' said Todd, and everyone smothered laughter.

'My grandmother has been vomiting all day,' the younger woman said into the silence. 'She doesn't seem to be able to stop.'

With great difficulty they ushered the pair into an empty

cubicle. Sophie left Leah with them as she went to gather the paperwork.

'Hello, Sophie.'

She looked up to find Daniel standing on the other side of the desk in his navy blue paramedic overalls. They fitted him superbly, the stripes on his shoulders completing the image of a professional intensive care paramedic. He had started work a few days ago.

Daniel swallowed hard and forced his facial features into neutrality as his body reacted to seeing Sophie in her uniform. It had been years since he had seen her dressed as a nurse. He remembered how it had turned him on, the virginal, don't-touch-me aura that the pristine white uniform had given her. It had made him want to get her dirty and the front zipper had always been too much of a temptation for him.

His eyes were drawn to the way the white cotton pulled across her bust and how her fob watch swung lazily across the fabric at her breast with each movement. It was hypnotising, the swish and sway mesmerising.

'Daniel,' she said, surprised. She knew that their paths were bound to cross at work from time to time but she hadn't been prepared to see him tonight.

The patient on the trolley coughed and Sophie remembered that there was actually a purpose to Daniel being here.

'Beryl!' Sophie recognised Daniel's patient instantly. She was a regular to the department and one of Sophie's favourites. Beryl had been Sophie's first-ever patient as a student nurse and she had nursed her on and off ever since.

'Hello…my…lovely.'

Beryl's speech was forced out between snatched breaths.

She sat bolt upright on the trolley, leaning forward slightly, her outstretched neck reminding Sophie of a turtle. An oxygen mask was pressed desperately by one shaky hand to her face.

She looked pale and pasty with a film of sweat on her creased forehead. Her eyes were large and round—fear of dying bulging them to their full extent. She clutched Sophie's hand across the desk. 'In…a…bad…way,' she said.

'Cube three,' she said to Daniel, and followed them into the cubicle.

Sophie busied herself getting Beryl settled while Daniel relayed the incident details and his treatment. Sophie tuned into the low rumble of his voice and her mind drifted to how she had loved to listen to him talk after they had made love and her head had been snuggled on his chest, her ear pressed to his skin.

'Sophie?'

She looked at Daniel blankly. Had he said something? He held the end of the oxygen tubing towards her and she stared at him for a few seconds before she realised he wanted her to plug it into their wall supply. She took it, feeling foolish, lecturing herself on appropriate workplace thoughts. She connected it and placed a finger probe on Beryl to assess her oxygen saturations.

She noticed the yellow staining on her patient's clubbed fingertips and the cigarette packet hanging out of Beryl's open handbag. It didn't take a genius to figure out what had been the cause of this acute exacerbation of her chronic airway disease.

'Beryl,' she chided gently, 'I thought you were giving up after your last scare.'

'Too old…too…set in my…ways,' Beryl wheezed. 'I'm old… I need some…pleasure.'

Pleasure. The word settled between them. Sophie looked at Daniel. Daniel looked at Sophie. Then they both looked away, busying themselves. Todd entered the cubicle and stood close to Sophie. She'd never been more grateful to see another human being. She beamed at Todd and relayed the information to him, tuning Daniel out altogether. When Daniel took his leave she almost sagged to the floor in relief.

Daniel pushed the trolley to the waiting ambulance, refusing to dwell on what had just happened inside. He helped the crew of the transport vehicle to restock and talked with them briefly about Beryl's case. He waved to them as they departed then climbed into his own single-officer vehicle.

The white Jeep was a compact mini emergency department equipped with almost everything he could ever require in any situation. Two people could be seated in the front but it was strictly a non-transport vehicle. IC paras were there to provide a higher skill set. Their cars were not equipped for patient transport.

As he drove out of the ambulance bay he remembered how Sophie had smiled at Todd and had seemed to only have eyes for him. Were they in a relationship? His mother hadn't mentioned anything in her regular phone calls and she'd always given him the rundown on Sophie and Max's goings on.

They were obviously very friendly, but was there something else going on? He felt sick. It had been bad enough thinking about Michael touching her, but this Todd guy? He was just too damn cute!

Back at St Jude's, Sophie didn't have time to reflect as Beryl kept them busy for a while. She was requiring regular Ventolin nebuliser treatments to improve the wheeze. A chest X-ray didn't show any new changes but it did reveal a slightly enlarged heart.

'Keep the nebs up every fifteen minutes to start with,' Todd ordered, scribbling on Beryl's bed chart. 'If she starts to become less short of breath, we'll knock it back.' He smiled at Sophie with his thousand-watt smile.

'I'll just reduce her oxygen now her saturations are in the mid-nineties,' Sophie said as she switched the neb mask for the oxygen one.

'Good idea. We don't want to knock off her respiratory drive.'

People with chronic airway disease operated on a hypoxic drive. The general population depended on rising carbon-dioxide levels in the bloodstream to stimulate a breath. Chronic airway sufferers had persistently elevated levels as their norm. Their bodies compensated for this by reverting to falling oxygen levels to stimulate a breath. Too much high-concentration oxygen could knock off this vital drive and the patient could just stop breathing.

'Nurse…Nurse.' Beryl clutched Sophie's arm and then the lapel of her uniform in a bid to bring Sophie closer.

'It's OK, Beryl, I'm here,' Sophie reassured her patient.

'I'm scared,' the old lady gasped out.

'Beryl, we've got you now.' Sophie softened her voice and spoke gently, trying to ease her favourite patient's distress. 'I know your breathing is difficult at the moment, but you are improving. Try not to panic, it'll just make your breathing worse.'

Beryl gulped in air like a fish floundering on the shore after it had been hooked. She fixed Sophie with frightened eyes. 'I don't…want to…die.'

Sophie squeezed Beryl's hand as Todd left the cubicle.

'That's just what I mean, Beryl. You need to think positively here. Come on, breathe with me. In…' Sophie sucked in a deep breath and held it. 'Now out…' she said, exhaling slowly. She repeated the exercise with Beryl, who quickly calmed down.

Half an hour later Sophie left the cubicle, satisfied that Beryl had settled. She gathered paperwork at the nurses' station.

'How's Beryl doing?' asked Todd.

'Better now.'

This time anyway. Both of them knew that Beryl was smoking herself to death. Today had been a close call and unfortunately they were becoming more and more frequent. One day soon she wouldn't be so lucky. Sophie hoped it wouldn't happen on her shift.

Two hours later Beryl's condition had stabilised and she was happy to go home. Her breathing had settled back to its normal level and her husband had arrived with her home oxygen cylinder for the trip back. As Sophie waved them off she wondered how long it would be until she saw Beryl again.

Sophie's thoughts were distracted by raised voices behind the curtain in cubicle four. It was the old lady in full swing again, pointing and swearing in Polish. Mrs Schmidt had vomited down her shirt and Leah was trying to remove the putrid clothing and put her into a fresh gown.

The old lady clutched at her top, ignoring the desperate pleas of Anna, her granddaughter, to let them help.

'I'm so sorry,' Anna apologized. 'My grandmother was in a refugee camp after the war. She has dementia now and thinks she's still back in the camp.'

Leah and Sophie looked at each other. Sophie didn't need to ask to know that Leah would be thinking the same thing. How awful to lose your mind and be stuck in an era that would have been dreadful enough the first time around. It would be like constantly reliving your worst nightmare.

They let the old woman be for a moment and her rantings stopped—temporarily. She continued to eye them suspiciously. Sophie's heart went out to Anna. She looked embarrassed and…exhausted.

'Does she live with you?' she asked.

'Yes. My grandfather died two years ago just as she was getting a bit forgetful. My husband and I have been looking after her ever since. The last few months have been very difficult with a new baby and all.'

'Does she have any periods of lucidity?' Leah asked.

'Not any more.'

Tears welled in Anna's eyes and she brushed them away quickly. Sophie put her arm around the young woman's shoulders and gave them a squeeze—she looked at her wits' end.

'Come on,' she said. 'Leah and I will change your grandmother and then we'll discuss getting her admitted and having her assessed by the geriatric assessment team.'

'But they'll put her in a home,' Anna sobbed. 'I promised Papa I'd look after her. I don't want her to be with strangers.'

'It doesn't have to come to that,' Sophie reassured her. 'They can help with all sorts of things—medication and respite and helping you with adapting your home for her needs.'

'Papa would never forgive me if I put her in a home.'

Sophie was moved by Anna's loyalty. 'Does she recognise you at all these days?'

'No,' the girl sniffed. 'She thinks she's in the camp. It wasn't a particularly pleasant place and she thinks I'm one of the guards.' Anna started to sob and Sophie comforted her a bit more.

'Hey, come on, now, we're going to need you to help us. Does your grandmother speak any English?'

'She used to be able to but she hasn't recognised it for about the last six months.'

'Well, we'll need you to translate. Talk to her and tell her what we're doing. It might help.'

'OK, Mrs Schmidt,' said Leah, 'time to get you cleaned up.'

They operated as a team, trying to remove Mrs Schmidt's blouse and dodge her fists as well. She fought and yelled and flailed her arms and hurled insults at the top of her lungs.

It was difficult work but Sophie had dealt with worse. She could only imagine the old woman's fright as she battled with her would-be attackers. She had to wonder, as Mrs Schmidt fought them tooth and nail, what kind of memory she was stuck in now.

It would have been comical had it not been so sad. One wizened old lady fighting off two nurses with a strength that belied her bird-like size and a mouth a wharfie would have been proud of. She may have been speaking Polish but everyone in the cube got the gist!

What happened next took Sophie completely by surprise. Afterwards she couldn't even recall how it had unfolded. Sophie turned to say something to Anna and as she turned back Mrs Schmidt's open hand connected with Sophie's face and knocked her backwards into the wall.

'Mama!' gasped Anna, yelling at her in Polish.

Sophie felt the wall behind her as she slid down it, cradling her stinging face and tasting the metallic taste of blood in her mouth.

'Sophie!' Leah rushed to her side. 'Are you OK?'

'Not really, no,' Sophie muttered, as stars floated in front of her eyes.

Leah poked her head out of the curtain. She couldn't see Todd but she did spy Daniel with a patient in tow, who was talking to Karen at the triage desk. 'Good. You'll do.' And she dragged him behind the curtain.

The noise in the cubicle was the first thing Daniel noticed. The elderly woman on the trolley was yelling in a strange language and the younger woman was yelling back at her between bouts of hysterical sobbing.

Then he noticed Sophie crouched on the floor and his heart almost stopped. She looked pale and shocked and he noticed the livid red mark on her face not adequately covered by her hand. He forgot all his angst and responded to her as he had always done when she had hurt herself, helping her up from the floor.

'Daniel?' Sophie looked at him, surprise adding to her dazed look.

He led her gently out of the cubicle.

'I'm OK, really,' said Sophie, the stars and buzzing noise starting to clear from her head. 'It was my fault. I wasn't quick enough. I didn't duck quick enough.'

Daniel sat Sophie on a chair in the staffroom, gently pried her fingers from her injured face and inspected the damage. 'You were assaulted, Sophie,' said Daniel testily. 'It wasn't your fault.' He probed her jaw and cheekbone and she grimaced slightly. 'Do you have ice packs?'

'Fridge,' she said, pointing to it.

Relieved to be moving away from her, he opened the door and retrieved an ice pack from the freezer. Sophie winced slightly as he knelt before her again and applied the chilled pack to the angry red mark.

'Put your teeth together and smile at me,' he said.

'I'm all right, Daniel,' she protested.

'Smile,' he reiterated, his blue eyes brooking no argument.

She did as she was told. 'Doesn't appear to be any major malformation. You should get an X-ray just in case, though.'

As he spoke he traced the outline of the ugly red weal with his fingertips. Back and forth. Back and forth. Sophie realised how close he was to her and found the caress hypnotising. Staring into his blue eyes as his fingers lightly stroked her aching face was compelling. She almost sighed as the faint touch took her back four years.

Todd rushed into the room and broke up the intimate scene. He all put pushed Daniel aside, repeating the quick checks he had just completed.

Daniel's earlier misgivings about Todd intensified. He felt the unnatural urge to pick the doctor up and throw him across the room as he watched Todd's fingers touching Sophie's face.

'We'll get an X-ray,' Todd said.

'No,' said Sophie rising from the chair. She was feeling

better now, her cheek just a dull ache. 'I'm fine. Nothing's broken. I'm just going to sport a shiner for a few days.'

'He's right,' Daniel butted in, the admission rankling. 'An X-ray would be sensible.'

'If I had an X-ray for every time a patient has whacked me, I'd be glowing green by now,' Sophie said dismissively.

'This happens a lot?' Daniel couldn't believe what he was hearing.

'More often than you think,' she admitted.

'That's appalling!'

'What are you going to do, Daniel? The majority of incidences occur with demented patients. Mrs Schmidt thinks she's in a refugee camp. I'm more cranky with myself than anything. I'm pretty good at ducking and weaving. I was silly for not being more on guard.'

Todd's pager went off. 'I have to go,' he said.

'Todd, make sure you document in Mrs Schmidt's chart that she needs her dementia assessed by the geriatric team.'

'Are you sure you'll be all right? I feel a little guilty about leaving,' he said, and pouted dramatically.

Sophie smiled and rolled her eyes as she sat back down. 'I'm fine. Go!' she ordered.

Daniel could have cheered when Todd left. He knelt before Sophie and placed his hand over hers as she cradled the ice pack to her cheek. He gently drew her hand away to inspect the injury. It was looking better. 'You'll live,' he said gruffly.

'Thank you, Daniel,' she said, because she had to say something to hide the confusion she was feeling.

They stared at each other for a few moments. His blue eyes compelling. His short, salt and pepper hair tempting.

His clean-shaven jawline strong and somehow comforting. Now thirty-one, Sophie had to admit he'd aged well. In fact, if anything, he looked better now, like he'd grown into his face.

Daniel became aware of his body's response to her closeness and quelled the reaction from years of practice. Her stare meant nothing. It was probably the way she stared at everyone. Probably the way she stared at Todd. No. Don't think about Todd.

'How's Beryl?' he asked huskily.

'We discharged her a little while ago. She'll be fine until next time. She's such a darling.'

Daniel heard the obvious affection in her voice and worried about her professional perspective where this particular patient was concerned. 'You do know, Sophie, that one day soon, especially if she continues irritating her airways with cigarette smoke, she's going to come in here and she'll die?'

'Of course, Daniel,' she said, annoyed at his statement of the obvious. 'So does she. That's why she's so scared.'

'Well, are you going to be OK with that?' he queried. 'I thought health-care workers were supposed to maintain a professional distance?'

'What are you saying, Daniel? Are you trying to tell me I don't know how to do my job?' She pushed him aside as she got up from the chair. She found herself angry again as four years of resentment bubbled to the surface.

'I think you may be too close to her, yes. As a nurse, I think you should know the dangers of that better than anyone.'

'I'm well aware of my professional boundaries, thank you very much. But sometimes the odd patient slips under the radar and, yes, I do have a soft spot for Beryl. You can think that's terrible if you like, but personally I believe it separates the good nurses from the great nurses. And I'm a bloody great nurse, Daniel. Not that you would know.'

'What's that supposed to mean?' he asked quietly.

'It means don't lecture me on my professionalism when you don't know the first thing about me. Don't jet off to the other side of the world and waltz back in from time to time and think you deserve to pass judgement on how I do my job.'

He heard the barely suppressed anger in her voice as her chest rose and fell. Rose and fell. 'Well, pardon me for caring,' he said sarcastically. 'There was a time when you used to care about what I thought, valued my opinion.'

'Oh, so now you care? Is that right, Daniel?'

'I've always cared, Sophie,' he sighed.

'Well, that's not what you said four years ago.'

Four years ago he'd said what he'd said to make sure she would fall into Michael's arms. And she had. Had been in them all along apparently. Max was proof of that. 'You recovered quickly enough,' he reminded her, a hard edge to his voice.

She gasped, stunned at the accusation. He had told her to marry Michael, to be with Michael. 'At least Michael knew how to love. Was capable of it,' she said bitterly.

'Sophie.' Leah called her name as she bustled into the room, stopping dead when she realised she'd obviously interrupted something. 'Everything OK in here?'

'Fine,' said Sophie smiling an overbright smile at her friend and then wincing as a sharp pain tore through the swelling on her cheekbone. 'I was just leaving.'

Sophie left the room with Leah with as much dignity as she could muster. Her body was quaking by the time she reached the desk. The gall. The absolute gall of the man to land back in her life and tell her how to do her job!

And for him to accuse her of rushing straight from his arms to Michael's. How dared he? He had practically offered her on a platter to his brother and now he was angry with her that she had done as he'd wanted?

Or was he just angry that she had thrown herself into it with one hundred per cent commitment? She had loved Michael. Had always loved him. She may not have fallen in love with him but he had been her best friend and confidant. Becoming his wife had seemed the most natural thing in the world when he had needed her so much and she had needed a father for Max.

And she was damned if she would be hanged for it!

CHAPTER THREE

SOPHIE woke with a start on Saturday morning to discover Max, who had got into bed with her at five a.m., was gone. It was now seven. Where was he? It was unusual for him to stir and for her not be aware of it. She must have been more tired than she'd thought. She hadn't got away from her shift last night until close to midnight and her feet had throbbed and her calves had ached as she had fallen into bed.

'Max,' she called out, presuming he would just be playing in their suite of rooms somewhere. No answer. He was probably watching the morning cartoons, she decided as she dragged herself out of bed and headed for the sitting room. TV off, no sign of Max.

John. He would be with John. Sophie quickly threw on her red gown with the large Chinese dragon embroidered on the back. She tightened the belt around her waist, ensuring her skimpy thong and tight T-shirt were fully covered.

It was too hot at this time of the year to wear anything but the bare minimum of clothes to bed. It was only because of Max that she wore anything at all—it wasn't that she hid her nudity from her son but a three-year-old's curiosity could be exhausting!

She walked briskly down the hallways. John wasn't quite up to his regular morning visit from Max. It was a routine that they had fallen into and John had loved his early morning wake-up calls. Max would take a book and climb in next to his G.G., snuggling into the crook of his arm, and John would make his great-grandson giggle with his silly voices.

She stopped at John's door and peered through the small gap created by the door having been left slightly ajar. She could see John's sleeping form and hear him snoring. No Max. Relief that he hadn't disturbed John didn't last long. If Max wasn't there, where was he?

She heard Max's high-pitched giggle coming from further down the hallway and followed the joyous sound to…Daniel's door. Great! She heard the low rumble of Daniel's voice and gave up all hope of being able to extract her son from the room without Daniel noticing.

She waited outside for a few moments, gathering the courage to enter. Something was obviously very funny. It sounded as if Max was being tickled if his squeals of delight were anything to go by. She didn't want to see what waited for her behind the door. Coward, she admonished herself. It can't be that bad.

She knocked quietly and opened the door slowly. It was. It *was* that bad, and more! A shirtless Daniel was throwing Max up in to the air and catching him again in smooth easy movements. Max was laughing so hard they hadn't even heard her enter. It was such an endearing picture Sophie felt her heart contract with love. To see her son with his father was way beyond anything she had words for.

'Mummy!' said Max, finally spying Sophie by the door. 'Dan's throwing me in the air!'

'Uncle Dan,' she corrected automatically, and then felt guilty at her deceit. The secret she had kept for four years suddenly weighing heavily on her.

Daniel stopped his activity and plonked a protesting Max on the bed beside him. She was wearing his gown. The one he had bought her for her twenty-first birthday. Back when they had made love at every opportunity and she had worn it with nothing underneath.

He drew his legs up beneath the sheet, tenting it to hide his quick reaction to the mental image that had flashed on his inward eye. His chest heaved a little still from the energy it had taken to repeatedly throw Max and then catch him. His arm muscles were already protesting the exercise.

She looked beautiful this morning. Her blonde hair all messed up and her sleepy eyes regarding him warily. The belt of the gown emphasised her small waist and even the T-shirt that peeked out from the V of the gown wasn't enough to disguise her braless state.

'Again, Unca Dan, again,' said Max, climbing onto Daniel's chest and straddling it. 'Giddy-up, Unca Dan.' He laughed, riding Daniel like a horse.

Daniel's gaze unlocked from hers as he turned his attention back to Max and made a clippity-clop noise with his tongue and bounced Max up and down.

'I'm sorry,' Sophie said, dragging her gaze away from his half-naked chest and finding her voice. 'I hope he didn't wake you.'

'I was dozing,' he said dismissively, not looking at her.

'Come on, Max. Let's leave Uncle Daniel to get some more sleep.'

'Oh, Mum. Dan's fun,' Max said, and continued his ride.

'He's OK,' Daniel assured her, concentrating on giving Max the bumpiest ride he could.

She stood there awkwardly. They hadn't seen each other since their heated discussion two nights ago and she was conscious of the strain between them.

'I…I thought you'd be at work by now,' she said, casting around for conversation.

'I start nights tonight.'

'Oh.' Nights! He was working nights? And she had a ride-along scheduled for tonight. Was there some conspiracy going on somewhere to deliberately throw them together? John's stroke. Charlie's emergency. How were they supposed to spend twelve hours together in the close confines of an ambulance?

'Problem?' he asked, finally looking at her.

'I'm rostered to do a ride-along tonight.'

Silence enveloped them. Daniel had stopped being a horse and Max seemed content to just sit on his uncle's chest. Damn it! He had known an RN was rostered on with him tonight; he'd just never thought it would be Sophie.

'Oh,' he replied.

'I'm hungry, Mummy.'

Grateful for the interruption, Sophie focussed on Max. 'Why don't you go down to the kitchen and see what Sally can fix you? Mummy will be there in a minute.' There were things to say if they were going to get through their shift together.

'Okey-dokey,' chirped Max, giving Daniel's abs one last giddy-up before scrambling off the bed and tearing out of the room.

'Are we going to be OK tonight or should I try and reschedule?' Sophie didn't see any point in beating about the bush. If he didn't think they could work together, she'd rather know now. Ride-alongs were notoriously difficult to switch due to advanced ambulance rostering. She wouldn't be popular with the ambulance brass if she interfered with their tightly run ship.

'I'm sure we're both mature enough to put our differences aside for a night. Right?'

Did he think she wouldn't be able to? 'I can if you can,' she said testily.

'Good. Well, I'll see you tonight. Shall we go together or take two cars?'

Sophie paused. It made perfect sense to take just one car. They were both going to the same place and had to be there at the same time. But something held her back. At least if she had her own car she could escape if she needed to. Why she would need to escape she wasn't quite sure, but car-pooling seemed a little intimate. They *had* to share the ambulance—there was no choice in that matter. But she did have a choice over this and the idea of having space from him appealed to her.

'Let's each get there under our own steam.'

He looked at her wordlessly and nodded his head. If that was what she wanted, so be it. He didn't want to think about it any more than he had to.

She turned to go.

'You're still wearing my gown.'

Sophie's heart slammed hard in her chest as her hand stilled on the doorframe. His gown. She blushed as she remembered the times she had spent with him in and out of the red floor-length gown. 'This old thing?' she said, keeping her voice deliberately light. 'I've had it for ages.'

'I know,' he said, his blue eyes boring into hers. 'I bought it for you. Don't you remember?'

She laughed, forcing the shaky note from her voice. 'Really? Goodness, I'd forgotten all about that.'

'Your twenty-first birthday present.'

She shook her head and smiled at him blankly.

'You put it on for me after the party and we made love with you still wearing it.' He couldn't believe she could have forgotten it. The gown, or what had happened later.

Sophie swallowed as she remembered the magical night. The night they had made love for the first time. It was one of her most treasured memories. She could only hope that if she ever got dementia, like poor Mrs Schmidt, it would be a memory that she could hold onto for ever. But for now it was better to play dumb. To pretend that the events of that night were so distant she could barely recall them.

'I think dredging up the past is kind of pointless. A lot of water has flowed under the bridge since then. I'll see you at seven o'clock.'

She turned on her heel and walked out of the room on very shaky legs. He had recognised the gown. She hadn't even realised its significance when she'd thrown it on but, then, she hadn't expected to be talking to Daniel in it either. He had been really pushing her to recall the memories. Why? What was the point? Nothing would change the past and, as they had both categorically stated, they were over each other.

Daniel brooded over the past as he checked his watch and absently stirred his coffee. She'd be here any minute.

He tried to be calm about it and sucked in a breath to dispel the disappointment he felt over her vagueness that morning.

Surely she hadn't really forgotten that he had given her the gown and the times he had pulled the belt to reveal her naked body beneath it? She had to be lying. Or had their time together come to mean so little? Had he hurt her that badly by rejecting her love four years ago that she had erased the memories from her mind for ever?

Such thoughts were going to get him nowhere but crazy! He must at all costs think of her and treat her as just another nurse riding along for the shift. Just another nurse.

Not as Sophie, his Sophie, Sophie of the dragon gown, Sophie his first and only love. But Sophie his sister-in-law. Sophie whose pinched and distraught face at Michael's funeral had haunted him. Sophie who had broken down as he had presented the eulogy, her sobs chilling him to the core. Because that Sophie was out of bounds!

Sophie drove to the inner-city ambulance station with some apprehension. How was she going to spend the next twelve hours in Daniel's company? The thought of awkward silences and loaded conversations was too awful to contemplate. She had the feeling that something was about to give and it was going to be ugly.

Maybe a pre-emptive strike was called for? Sure, they had talked about the incident after Michael's funeral but had steadfastly ignored all their other history. And they had history to burn! Lots of highs and some pretty awful lows.

She had spent a lot of the last four years being angry with him. And where had it got her? On a ride-along, that's where. So maybe it was time to let bygones be bygones. Be the bigger person, acknowledge the past and move on.

They didn't have to spend hours pulling everything to pieces, psychoanalysing every word, every action. They could just admit that the past was part of their lives so they could get on with their futures.

She came to a decision as she parked the car and shut her door firmly. She would talk to him about it. First thing. Clear the air. Agree to start anew, whether they liked it or not!

Once inside the building she pushed open the door that said INTENSIVE CARE PARAMEDIC SERVICES. It opened quietly and she spied Daniel immediately. He was standing in the small kitchen area, seemingly engrossed in the contents of the mug he was stirring. He didn't hear her enter.

She took a moment to study him. His navy blue overalls fitted him snugly from the back. He was tall and lean. Taller than Michael even, who had been six feet. His uniform only hinted at the attributes she had witnessed that morning as he had played with Max. Broad shoulders, firm back sloping to a narrower waist.

His short back and sides hairstyle suited him. It looked spiky but she knew from experience it was actually soft and quite fine. The longer hair on top fell in soft layers and was peppered with grey highlights, brushing his forehead in a shortish fringe. He was as sexy as—there was no denying it.

'Are you trying to read your tealeaves?'

And then he turned around and smiled at her, holding her gaze easily. His eyes crinkled at the corners and Sophie was drawn to the grey at his temples. The smile tipped her off balance. She hadn't expected it after that morning's conversation. It seemed as unfettered as his smiles of old.

'Come in,' he said, breaking eye contact. 'I'll show you around.'

She walked towards him and he braced himself for the impact of her nearness. Her perfume floated his way, reaching him before she did, and he felt as if an invisible tentacle had shimmered forward and wrapped itself around his waist.

'This is it, I'm afraid. It's not very big.' He gestured around him.

Sophie had to agree. The room was tiny. Most paramedics worked out of large city or suburban stations but because there were so few IC paras they only got a small-ish room situated at Ambulance Service Headquarters.

There was a kitchenette, a toilet and shower and a lounge area that housed two recliner chairs, a large-screen television and video.

He showed her where to stash her bag and handed her a fluorescent pop-over vest with OBSERVER emblazoned on the back and front in reflective lettering.

'What happens now?' she asked.

'Make yourself a cuppa and have a seat. It's all a waiting game from now on. Saturday nights are pretty busy but it doesn't usually hot up until after ten.'

She followed his advice and sat in the recliner next to him. She feigned interest in the TV sports show he seemed to be engrossed in. She sipped at her tea and formulated the words she would say to end this awkwardness. She despaired at the kind of night she was going to have if he continued to ignore her like this.

Daniel gripped the arms of the chair and kept his face turned forward. If he looked at her he might not want to stop. He could feel her presence to the left of him like an encroaching force field. Every movement she made rippled the energy closer and closer. Soon he would be totally swallowed up by it and every cell in his body screamed, *danger!*

Sophie could bear it no longer. She had to clear the air. 'Daniel.'

'Mmm?' he said, his eyes not leaving the screen.

And then she chickened out. Her carefully planned speech dried in her throat. This wasn't going to be as easy as she'd thought! 'Do you think I could have a look in the ambulance? I know the IC para cars are different to the standard ones and I'd like to familiarise myself with the layout if I'm going to be of any use to you tonight.'

He leapt up, pleased for the opportunity to put some distance between them. 'Good idea.' He nodded. 'This way.'

Daniel opened the door that led to the outside world and the white two-seater Jeep sitting idle in the driveway. Red reflective lettering that read INTENSIVE CARE PARAMEDIC decorated the side panels and the bonnet. The ambulance service crest was on both doors. The red beacons on the roof completed the look.

'The supplies are in the back here,' Daniel announced as he opened up the doors and stepped back to allow for their outward swing.

Sophie inspected the equipment, all stowed on special shelves and securely fastened. A Lifepak that doubled as a heart monitor and defibrillator was in easy reach. There was also portable oxygen and suction apparatus, a large orange box full of drug ampoules and IV therapy supplies.

Several pre-packed bundles, sterilised and single use, were also available. A chest tube pack, a maternity pack, a tracheostomy pack and a trauma kit. There was also a soft-sided, multi-pocketed bag full of dressing and bandage supplies.

Cervical collars and splints were in special net holders attached to the interior roof. A spinal board ran down the center, reaching right down between the front bucket seats.

'It's well equipped,' Sophie commented, turning to face him.

He nodded. 'What we don't carry the standard ambulances do. IC paras usually get despatched as code-two back-ups. Rarely are we first on scene. More often than not they stand us down once the first crew on scene assesses the situation and calls in their sitrep.'

'The cases you do attend, what do they usually involve?'

'We're mainly used for IV access or pain relief. IC paras are the only paramedic level that carries narcotics so we do a lot of those kinds of jobs. Occasionally we get a big multi-trauma or intubation, something that really tests our skills.'

'It must be very different from your last job. I'd imagine even on its worst Saturday night ever, the streets of Brisbane are chicken feed compared to New York.'

'Oh, yeah.'

He laughed and his eyes crinkled, and it took Sophie back to her childhood. When he would beat her at chess and her crankiness would amuse him.

'But, still, I don't mind the slower pace. You so often don't get time to even think properly over there. You just react. It's all go, go, go. And it's nice, living in a city where violence isn't a way of life.'

Sophie was surprised to gain this small insight into his

life over the last few years. They'd not spoken about anything personal since his return. Maybe this was a good opening to discuss their issues.

But his pager had other ideas as it interrupted with its insistent beep, beep, beep. She watched as he pulled it off his belt clip and scrolled through the message.

'House fire out at Sunvalley. You ready?' he asked.

She nodded and watched as he shut the back doors and briskly got into the Jeep. She donned her pop-over vest and climbed in next to him.

'Coms, this is unit 001.' Daniel spoke into the handheld radio hanging off the centre console.

Sophie noticed how his full lips were pressed to the black plastic of the microphone as he spoke.

'Unit 001, have you proceeding to a house fire at number six Riverbed Drive at Sunvalley. Map reference 102 Lima twelve. You'll be backing up unit 990. The fire service reports unknown casualties at this stage. Proceed code two, pending sitrep. The Sunvalley first responder group will also be attending.'

'Roger that, Coms.'

They drove in silence for a while, each preparing mentally for what they might find when they arrived on scene.

'What is the first responder group Coms was talking about?' asked Sophie.

'It was an initiative by the ambulance service to provide for the more remote parts of Brisbane where response times can be delayed. They're volunteers who have been trained and respond to accident and medical emergencies in their area.'

'Sounds like a good idea.'

'It's fantastic,' he agreed, enthusiasm evident in his voice. 'I've been out to a couple of jobs there already and they're a great bunch of people. Dedicated to their community.'

Sophie was about to respond when the radio crackled to life.

'Coms, this is unit 990. Two patients. One with minor injuries. The other with extensive burns. Can we have the IC upgraded to code one?'

'Roger, 990. Do you copy, 001?'

'Copy,' replied Daniel, flicking a switch on the dashboard that activated the beacons and siren as he accelerated quickly.

Sophie held on as the sirens wailed. Daniel thrust the Brisbane directory at her and ordered her to navigate. Ten minutes later they pulled up at the scene.

'Sophie, grab the dressing and IV kit,' he said as they alighted from the vehicle. 'I'll get the drugs and the Lifepak.'

Sophie had put on her clinical mask, as had Daniel. The seriousness of the situation had banished her feelings of unease. At least in this arena they were on a level playing field.

They rushed to the badly burnt man and received a brief handover from the paramedics already on scene. One of the first response team had placed a sterile burns sheet over the victim and was dousing it with water, while another held an oxygen mask close to the man's badly burnt face. The man was groaning and shaking quite visibly beneath the sheet.

'Let's pull the sheet back so we can assess the damage,' suggested Daniel, and nodded to Larry, one of the responders, who gently peeled it back.

Sophie swallowed the gasp that rose in her throat. The

burns were extensive. The patient's clothes had been burnt away, leaving the charred flesh exposed. It looked like it had been peeled back in places and was all red and fleshy. Mostly, however, it was quite black—charred.

The man's entire front had borne the full fury of the fire. His chest, abdomen, groin and legs had all been burned. His face didn't look as bad—maybe only superficial burns—but the rest looked partial to deep thickness to Sophie.

'Anything on his back?' Daniel asked Larry.

'Nothing,' he confirmed.

Poor guy, Daniel thought as he did a quick calculation in his head, using the rule of nines, an internationally recognised system for estimating the extent of a patient's burns. Fifty to sixty per cent, Daniel calculated quickly.

He nodded to Larry to replace the sheet and to continue the water treatment.

'What's your name, mate?' Daniel asked the patient.

'Simon,' he croaked.

'I'm Daniel. I'm a paramedic. This is Sophie. How's your pain, Simon?'

'It hurts real bad.'

'Right. What I'll do is put a couple of intravenous lines in and give you some morphine. We'll also start some fluids and get you to hospital as quick as we can. OK?'

'Whatever. Just hurry!'

'Sophie, get a line in that side,' he ordered. 'I'll get one this side.'

Thankfully Simon's arms were relatively unscathed so finding a vein wasn't going to be too difficult. Still, she felt a pressure to get it right the first time. One thing Simon needed more than anything at this moment, even getting to hospital, was fluid.

She'd seen a lot of major burns patients in her time and it was usually awful. But this? This was different again. Here, tending to the patient on the ground, in the dark, with the intense heat emanating from the smouldering house behind them, was a startling reality check.

There was a rawness about this scene that didn't exist in the hospital situation. When patients arrived at St Jude's they seemed…cleaner somehow. The freshness and the newness of the situation had ebbed and the real sense of urgency had dissipated. Back in the department things were clean and white and ordered. Here it was dark and dirty and messy.

This was real touch-and-go stuff, even more so than in the emergency department. What they did here could determine Simon's outcome. She shivered at the huge responsibility and wondered how Daniel did it day after day.

The needle slipped in easily and she ran a bag of fluid through a giving set and attached it, commandeering Larry to act as a human IV pole. She checked the ampoule of morphine with Daniel and he pushed it straight into the IV line.

'OK, Simon. The pain should start to ease off now,' Daniel assured him.

The thing Daniel had to worry about now was any respiratory involvement. He shone his penlight up Simon's nose and noted the singed nasal hairs. He'd obviously sustained some inhalation burn injury to his respiratory tract.

The extent was difficult to assess, looking from the outside. Simon's airway could be swelling right now. There was no audible respiratory stridor at the moment, which was a plus. But his voice had sounded croaky. They should load him and go. If he should need intubating, that was something better done at the hospital.

'Do you want the fluids running to the standard formula?' Sophie asked.

'Sure,' he said. 'I'll get the stretcher.'

One of the major problems with burns victims was the dramatic fluid shifts that went on inside their bodies. Fluid that usually circulated through their vessels was pushed out, into the interstitial spaces. It was imperative that this fluid be replaced and for further losses to be accommodated.

An international protocol governed the type and the amount of intravenous fluids to be given, depending on body weight, surface area, burns percentage and time elapsed since the initial injury.

As Sophie did the calculations, Daniel, with the help of the first responders and the other two paramedics, loaded Simon into the back of the ambulance. The second patient, who had sustained a minor burn to one hand, was also going with them.

Daniel handed the Jeep keys to Sophie. 'Follow us,' he said. 'We're going to St Jude's.'

Sophie's hand closed around the keys. Obviously Daniel was going to ride in the back of the ambulance with Simon and he wanted her to drive the Jeep.

The ambulance pulled away, light and sirens blazing. Sophie stopped to thank the first responders and then got in the Jeep and followed at a more sedate pace, listening to the radio chatter. She parked near the emergency doors on her arrival at St Jude's and found Daniel completing his paperwork in the back of the ambulance.

'How is he?' she asked.

'He's just developed a mild stridor. They're going to electively intubate him and send him to ICU.'

Fifteen minutes later Daniel had filled out his report form, restocked the Jeep, called himself clear at Coms and they were on their way back to Headquarters.

He watched Sophie surreptitiously and noticed how quiet she was, just sitting and staring out the window.

'You OK, Sophie?' he asked gently.

'Uh-huh.' She nodded and turned to face him. 'It's just…you know. Different.'

'What is?'

'Your job and mine. It's so…raw. You see people at the worst possible moments in their lives. At least when they get to us the initial shock has worn off and they're…I don't know, cleaner or something. Your job's pretty confronting.'

'It can be—sure,' he admitted, holding her gaze as he pulled up at a traffic light. She'd obviously been affected by Simon's case. Seeing him writhing on the ground, extreme pain racking his charred body, was about as raw as it got.

Sophie gazed into Daniel's blue eyes. Even in the semi-darkness of the car they glowed. He saw stuff like this all the time. How did he cope with it?

The pager beeped into the silence and she looked away, quickly reining in her emotions.

'Here we go again,' he murmured.

The next few hours flew by with no real chance to talk. They spoke about clinical things and directions and possible scenarios they might encounter. They communicated well on that level, comfortable with each other at last. They were despatched to seven cases and stood down from five.

Sophie felt dizzy from all the going back and forth and the turning around and the noise of the siren and the irritating strobing of the vehicle beacons. She was relieved when they finally got back to Headquarters.

'We should try and get some sleep,' Daniel said, passing her a blanket. 'There's no telling when we'll be needed next. It's nearly one a.m.'

Now they were alone again Daniel had slipped back into his awkwardness. She watched as he pushed his recliner back and dimmed the overhead lights, not looking at her once. He turned his back to her so he was lying on his side, facing the wall.

She'd enjoyed the last few hours. She'd never worked with him before and was surprised by their synchronicity. There had been an ease that had echoed past times. Their angst had been forgotten as they had worked like a team that had been together for years.

It seemed they could talk for hours about medical matters with no evidence of strain. Work side by side to save a patient's life, no problems. But now they were back at HQ, with no lives hanging in the balance, four years of baggage loomed large.

Sophie adjusted the blanket around her and got comfortable in the chair but she lay awake, unable to sleep.

'Daniel.' It was now or never.

'Yes, Sophie.' He didn't turn to face her.

'Truce?'

'I wasn't aware we were fighting,' he hedged, talking to the wall.

'We can't go on like this. We've got the rest of the shift to get through and I think for John's sake and your parents and even Max, we should be able to get along.'

Daniel squeezed his eyes tight and stifled a sigh. That was easier said than done when he only had to look at her and his emotions became tangled in such a bitter-sweet jumble he didn't know whether he wanted to spank her or kiss her.

'Daniel?'

He moved around in his chair until he was sitting properly and turned his head to look at her. 'Can we do that, Sophie? Can we put everything behind us? You were sleeping with my brother at the same time you were sleeping with me. Did you tell Michael you loved him as well or did you only save that particular honour for me?'

Sophie shut her eyes at the accusation in his voice. How could he think that of her? The denial came to her lips but she quashed the impulse to clear her character. There had been four years of lies trapping her in a web that just got stickier. She had let him think the worst because it was the only plausible explanation for Max.

'What do you care? You never loved me anyway.'

'See,' he whispered into the gloom. 'Difficult, isn't it?'

Sophie swallowed hard as his point hit home. 'Difficult, sure...but not impossible. If we just agree to leave the past where it belongs—'

'Ignore it, you mean?'

'No. Acknowledge that we have one but let the emotions go. I don't think we're ever going to get anywhere if we go ten rounds of I-said-you-said.'

He was silent for a few minutes, digesting her suggestion. Maybe she was right. It would make life a lot easier around the house. Of course he couldn't control where his mind wandered but he could control what came out of his mouth and the way he acted towards her. 'OK. Truce,' he agreed.

Sophie let out the breath she'd been holding. For the foreseeable future they would be living under the same roof—hopefully their agreement would ease the way.

The beeper went off an hour later as Daniel lay staring at the ceiling, still wide awake.

'What is it?' Sophie murmured sleepily.

'"Seventy-year-old female. Difficulty breathing. History of COAD,"' he read off the pager. 'Come on, sleepyhead.' He deliberately used a light teasing tone, rising quickly and grabbing her hand to pull her to her feet. 'Let's hustle.'

They got in the car and Daniel contacted Coms on the radio.

'Thank you, 001. You are proceeding to one hundred and fifty Peermont Road, Newfarm. Code one, please. You should be first unit on scene.'

'Roger,' said Daniel, and put the mike down. 'That's Beryl,' he said, urgency in his voice and actions as he switched the sirens on and planted his foot on the accelerator.

Sophie almost groaned. Just when they had found some common ground they were going to have to confront a situation that would once again put them at odds. Well, if he thought she was going to be anything other than herself with Beryl, he could think again! She wasn't going to be cool or distant because he disapproved of her relationship with a patient.

They arrived at Beryl's in just under five minutes. Sophie lugged the oxygen and Lifepak as Daniel came up behind with the drug box.

Beryl's husband ushered them through the door and Sophie was instantly aware of the ingrained odour of cigarette smoke. It permeated everything—the curtains, the carpets, the linen on her bed. No wonder her airways were constantly irritated.

Beryl was sitting bolt upright in bed, one leg over the side, her foot planted on the floor, pushing herself as far forward as possible. A Ventolin nebuliser misted out around the mask she was clutching to her face. She looked frightened. Not even the sight of Sophie erased the fear.

'Beryl,' Sophie said, going straight to her and swapping the oxygen tubing over to their cylinder and cranking it up. 'It's OK. We're here now,' she soothed.

Sophie quickly attached three electrodes to her patient's chest and switched on the Lifepak. The heart rhythm looked normal, albeit a little fast.

'Can't…breathe,' Beryl forced out, holding Sophie's hand desperately.

Sophie sat beside her on the bed and worked through the elderly woman's breathing with her. Beryl's hand was sweaty but Sophie didn't mind. She watched Daniel out of the corner of her eye and wondered what he was thinking. If this one small comfort helped ease her patient's fears, he could go to hell. Beryl's anxiety was only making her breathing worse. And besides, Sophie was a nurse, she comforted—that was her job!

Daniel busied himself with setting up an IV line just in case they needed it. Beryl seemed worse to him than she had the other day, snatching every breath she could. She was pale and clammy and as Sophie applied the BP cuff he also noticed she was hypertensive. They needed to get her to hospital pronto. If she were to go into respiratory arrest out here, he didn't fancy her chances.

The smell of cigarette smoke polluted the air inside the house and Daniel found his ire rising. Why did people do this to themselves? It was all well and good to say nicotine was addictive but surely not being able to breathe was a good incentive to kick the habit? Daniel despised smoking with a passion. He'd seen too many people like Beryl throw their lives away.

Sophie removed the nebuliser mask now that the dose was finished, put on a normal mask and delivered the oxygen at six litres per minute as Beryl's oxygen saturations weren't too bad. The urge to really crank it up was tempting but Sophie didn't want to confuse Beryl's hypoxic drive.

They heard the other ambulance arrive and Sophie went to meet them, instructing them to bring the stretcher, as they would be transporting as soon as possible.

Once again Sophie drove the Jeep to St Jude's behind the ambulance, pulling in simultaneously this time. Beryl had settled quite a bit on the brief ride to St Jude's, as was often the case. Patients' conditions could be exacerbated by their anxiety. The knowledge that they had a trained professional tending them and they were in good hands often had a beneficial effect.

'Good luck, Beryl.' Sophie squeezed her favourite patient's hand as Richard, who was on Triage, took her through to the cubicles.

Sophie waved to her until she disappeared behind the

curtains. She would be very sad when Beryl finally passed from this world. Daniel was right about that. But as much as it angered her that her favourite patient was smoking herself to death, Sophie knew that Beryl was a mature adult who understood what she was doing.

Todd came out from a nearby cubicle. 'Hey. Sophie. Wow! Sexy vest.'

She laughed and did a little pirouette. 'Oh, yes. Very glam!'

'It is on you, sugar doll. But, then, you'd look good in a sack.'

A sack? Or *the* sack. Daniel had heard their banter as he'd rounded the corner. It was obvious Todd had a major crush on Sophie. His tongue was hanging out a mile. The guy was just too smooth for Daniel's liking.

'Let's go,' he said, trying to keep the terse note out of his voice.

Daniel drove back to HQ, mulling over the Todd thing. Of course other men would find Sophie attractive. She wasn't exclusively available to Monday men after all. One day he supposed she would find someone else. It was easy to forget she was only twenty-five, she'd been around in his life for so long.

Snippets of memories flitted through his mind as he navigated the Jeep. The day he and Michael had first met her, a gawky, gangly five-year-old, sent to spend the school holidays at Arabella while her mother had recovered from depression. And the many other school holidays that had been the highlight of his younger years.

G., teaching them all to play chess, and the many games she'd insisted they play together so she could get good enough to beat him. The cake she had harangued Sally to let her cook for his sixteenth birthday, complete with a very wobbly DANIEL that her eleven-year-old fingers had personally iced. And…the red gown.

Daniel pulled up in the driveway of Headquarters and switched off the engine. OK, so he'd agreed to let the past go but…surely she hadn't really forgotten? The hours he had spent searching for just the right gown returned to him. The embarrassment of hanging out in lingerie departments. The shop assistant who had winked and taken pity on him, helping him to find exactly what he had been looking for.

'Daniel?'

Her quiet interruption brought him back to the present. He turned to face her and he knew he couldn't let it be.

'Are we going in?' she asked, looking at him oddly.

He looked at her some more, his intense blue gaze holding hers. Was that her breathing he could hear roughening? Was she licking her lips because they were dry or was she nervous or something else?

'Were you serious this morning about the gown?'

Sophie's breath stuttered out into the close confines of the Jeep. Must they talk about this again? She looked down into her lap. 'Daniel, I thought we agreed—'

He placed two fingers beneath her chin and turned her head towards him. She looked tired and wary and fragile and…beautiful.

'The gown, Sophie. Don't tell me you don't remember.'

'I…'

'I've pulled that belt so many times.'

'Stop it, Daniel,' she begged in a hoarse whisper. 'This just gets us nowhere.'

'Tell me you remember,' he insisted softly.

'No,' she said, shaking her head and dislodging his fingers, hardening the wobbly edge to her voice. 'I don't. I won't.' She had to deny it. If she admitted it now, if she put it out there, she feared that all their suppressed intimacy would be unleashed and overwhelm the tiny space that separated them.

He lifted her face again and he could see the determination glitter in her eyes.

'Tell me.'

She shook her head mutinously. Staring him down. Every cell rebelled at his request, screamed at her to get out, but there was something compelling about his eyes, his stare, that she couldn't resist.

Daniel felt his breathing roughen and fall into sync with hers. He knew if he didn't kiss her right now he was going to die.

But instead of being soft and gentle and giving, it was insistent, punishing. His fingers held her jaw steady as he plundered her mouth for a few brief seconds and then pulled away. 'Tell me,' he gasped.

'Go to hell,' she said through clenched teeth.

He lowered his head again and repossessed her soft lips, revelling in her resistance as she shook her head from side to side. They pulled apart again and the air seemed to crackle like a brooding sky before a thunderstorm. Their harsh breathing louder than a cyclonic wind. 'Say it and I'll stop.'

Her eyes grew large. He was seriously going to blackmail her over this? 'I remember,' she whispered, because she had to stop this craziness and she didn't think she could cope if he kissed her again.

But he kissed her again anyway. Softer this time. Slower. His fingers stroking her jaw, her cheek. 'What do you remember?'

She heard the pleading note in his voice and responded to it just as she always had. 'I remember that the gown was a gift from you,' she said quietly, leaning her forehead against his, 'and that I used to tease you by wearing nothing underneath it so you would pull the cord and take it off and make love to me.'

She felt the gentle kiss he pressed to her forehead and tears pricked at her eyes. Was he satisfied now?

'Thank you,' he whispered, kissing her forehead again.

They pulled apart and sat quietly, each staring out of the windscreen straight ahead, collecting their thoughts and letting their breathing settle.

What had possessed him? He didn't know. It had suddenly been so important to him for her to acknowledge their past. Their earlier decision to ignore it had made it seem all the more crucial. 'I'm sorry,' he said. 'I shouldn't have done that.'

'Damn right,' she said, reaching for the doorhandle and letting herself out.

She walked into the staffroom, collected her bag and was out of the door again as he was just alighting from the vehicle.

'Where are you going? Shift's not over yet.'

'It is as far as I'm concerned,' she threw over her shoulder, walking briskly to her car.

Daniel watched her leave, mentally berating himself for his stupidity. He hadn't meant for things to get so out of hand. They were supposed to be moving on. He'd acted impulsively and had really ticked her off.

Worse, their kiss had stirred something inside that he'd managed to put into deep freeze for four years. Maybe he wasn't as over her as he thought?

CHAPTER FOUR

MAX jumped on Sophie at four o'clock the next day. She didn't usually sleep this late after a night shift but she'd tossed and turned for hours, reliving the incident with Daniel before finally getting to sleep midmorning.

'Come on, Mummy. Wake up. You've been asleep for ages. It's Family Sunday.'

Sophie stretched and woke to find eyes as blue as Daniel's staring back at her.

'Helwo, Mummy,' said Max smiling at her.

'Hello, my Maxster,' said Sophie.

'I wuv you, Mummy,' he said.

'I love you, too.' She grinned and closed her eyes as Max stuck his thumb in his mouth and reached for a strand of her hair, rubbing it against his cheek. Max gave her another five minutes' sleep, indulging in a rare moment of tranquillity, the comfort of his old routine still having a calming effect. But the joys of Family Sunday beckoned.

'Mummy,' he whispered, opening one eye for her with a chubby finger.

'I'm coming,' she said, opening both eyes before Max did damage to her eyeball.

She got out of bed and threw on a pair of shorts and a T-shirt. Max left her to it, satisfied that she was up. She gave herself a once-over in her mirror. Her hair looked a little worse for wear so she scraped it up into a ponytail. Still average, but it would have to do.

She tried not to think about last night as she slowly made her way to the formal lounge room. Walking out on Daniel like that had been highly unprofessional but, then, so was what he had done. Kissing her like that—she could have him for sexual harassment, no contest!

'Afternoon everyone,' she said, suppressing a yawn as she joined the clan.

They were all there—John, Edward and Wendy, Sally and a fully recovered Charlie, Max and…Daniel. Someone had put a CD on and the light music was a perfect backdrop to the lively conversation.

Family Sunday was a Monday tradition that had been around for longer than Sophie had been on the scene. It involved the family coming together on Sunday afternoons and spending time with each other, afternoon cocktails and conversation leading to a wonderfully cooked dinner courtesy of Sally.

Wendy had introduced it when Michael and Daniel had been little to ensure there was one day in the week they all came together. A family of doctors didn't make for the most regular routine and as the boys had got older they, too, had had many activities that had taken them away from regular family time.

Sophie and Michael had continued it with Max. John had usually joined them, with Edward and Wendy there as well between jaunts on the European lecture circuit. And since John's stroke, Family Sunday was going stronger than ever.

Sophie accepted a glass of champagne from Edward and laughed at a joke Charlie was telling. She was reminded of happier times before Michael's accident when the family, no matter where they had been or what they had been doing had all tried to make it to Arabella for Family Sunday.

'Mummy,' Max said, running to her and hugging her around her legs, his little face beaming with excitement. Her son loved Family Sunday more than any of them. The fact that he was usually the centre of attention the obvious reason.

Sophie was excruciatingly aware of Daniel. She glanced at him over her champagne glass as he popped a roasted cashew into his mouth and looked directly at her. Was he angry about her storming off last night? He didn't seem to be.

Max headed for the bowl of nuts and Sophie picked them up out of his reach, placing them on the high table next to John.

'Oh, I want a nut, Mummy.' Max pouted.

'You're too little for nuts, Maxy. Have one of Sally's chocolate crackles instead,' she said, offering him the plate of assorted nibbles Sally had put out for everyone.

The next half-hour was full of laughter. Sophie had doubted she could laugh today with the events of last night still fresh in her mind, but the Monday family intimacy worked its magic. There was just something about being with people who knew you. Really knew you and loved you unconditionally.

Having John in his wheelchair brought a touch of *déjà*

vu to the proceedings. Michael had loved Family Sunday almost as much as Max. Looking around the room, it seemed strange that they were all together without him. It was hard to believe that it had been over two years since his death.

A squeal of pure delight interrupted her thoughts as Daniel lifted Max up onto his shoulders and jigged him up and down. Max giggled and held onto Daniel's head. She watched them together, noting the similarities between father and son. They had the same eyes and the same lazy smile. When Max cracked up at something funny it reminded her so much of Daniel's childhood chuckle that it almost took her breath away.

But that was pretty much where the similarities ended. In fact, in many ways he had looked much more like his uncle, which had made it easier for Michael to pass him off as his own. Looking at the four generations of Monday men present in the lounge, Sophie could see the strong family resemblance shared by all the men in the family. Yes. Max was definitely a Monday.

Sophie had promised Michael the day he'd proposed to her that she would never reveal the truth to Daniel. She had been hurt and angry at the time and Michael had been right when he'd said it would be too complicated. He had wanted to raise her baby as his and he had loved her and needed her and they had been best friends. It had been the perfect solution.

'Look at me, Mummy. Look at me,' said Max from his lofty perch. He stood on his father's shoulders now, stretched out to his full height, his chubby hands held firmly in Daniel's. The pure joy of being a child glowed in his eyes and she felt absurdly like crying. He definitely had his father's eyes.

'Yes, darling, look at you,' Sophie agreed, blinking back the tears that momentarily blurred her vision.

Daniel saw the shimmer of moisture in Sophie's eyes and frowned slightly. Was this about last night or just one of those things that made women such a mystery?

He remembered how sentimental she had always been.

How she cried at Anzac Day marches and got all misty-eyed whenever she saw a bride. In his teens he had enjoyed teasing her about it and had taken great delight in how huffy she would become and even more so when she would storm out in disgust. Just like she had last night.

He saw her blink rapidly and look away, and was grateful to Max who started to tap dance on his shoulder-blades, demanding to be put down. He aeroplaned his squealing nephew onto John's lap and watched with satisfaction as Max's little arms twined around the old man's neck. It reminded him of the many hours he had spent sitting in the same spot and how close he had always been to his grandfather.

Max whispered something in John's ear that made him laugh, and Daniel was pleased that John had this little boy's adoration to help him through the tough times. And for the first time in his life he felt a streak of envy.

Sophie was talking to Sally and Charlie when she heard Max coughing. She turned instinctively, a sixth sense shooting a tremor of unease through her gut. Max appeared to be choking, coughing and gasping, panic widening his eyes.

'Max!' Sophie leapt up and was at his side in seconds, plucking him off John's lap and slapping him on the back.

'What have you eaten, Maxy?' she demanded, slapping him some more as he continued to choke.

Sophie was shaking. Adrenaline surged through her system. Logically she knew that the obstruction should clear but this was her child and he couldn't breathe and he was looking at her in sheer terror.

'It must have been the nuts!' John's alarm said it all.

'He'll be right,' said Daniel, coming to Sophie's side, trying to be calm, hoping this would ease the gut-wrenching fright stamped on her face.

'He can't breathe, Daniel.' She turned to him, her dark blue eyes beseeching him as she watched the pink of Max's lips lose their colour.

'Call an ambulance, Mum,' he said pulling Max away from Sophie, who was crazily slapping her son's back. He felt confident that Max would clear his own airway soon enough but back-up wouldn't hurt. 'Dad, in my car boot is my kit. Grab it for me.'

Sophie watched Max's lips become dusky and his body go limp. Tears fell unchecked from her eyes. 'Please, help him, Daniel. Do something,' she yelled. She couldn't lose Max. She'd already lost her mother and Michael. The very thought made her frantic.

Daniel flipped his nephew over until his head was lying face down in Daniel's hand. He supported the little body with his forearm and then laid him along his extended leg. He administered several sharp blows to Max's back between his little shoulder blades. No luck.

'Ambulance is on its way,' Wendy said, running back into the room. She put her arm around Sophie, pulling her daughter-in-law close. 'He'll be OK,' she soothed. If any one knew the mind-numbing panic of losing a child, it was Wendy.

'It's been too long,' Sophie wailed. 'He should have coughed it out by now.'

Edward arrived with Daniel's bag. Daniel's heart thumped in his chest. He quashed the rising tide of despair and worry. If he let his emotions get in the way he'd be as useless as Sophie. Someone needed to take charge.

What he was doing wasn't working. He knew he had to take a look and see if he could remove the obstruction himself. Luckily he had the equipment to do so.

He laid Max's limp body on the floor.

'Here, Daniel,' said Edward, passing his son a laryngo-scope and Magill's forceps he'd found in Daniel's kit.

Daniel was grateful that his father also seemed to be keeping his head. As a renowned paediatric cardiologist, he certainly knew his way around the equipment.

'Hurry, Daniel,' Sophie begged, her voice holding an urgency that bordered on hysteria.

Daniel blocked it out. He blocked everything out and talked silently to Max. Don't do this to us, buddy. Mummy needs you. We all need you.

He opened Max's mouth and inserted the blade of the laryngoscope down the side of his tongue, extending Max's neck slightly as he manoeuvred the instrument to view his nephew's airway. The light source illuminated the small space well and he almost cheered when he located the of-fending nut occluding the trachea just past the epiglottis.

His father held the forceps by their angled neck for ease of transfer, and Daniel took them from him without even looking up. Everyone in the room held their breath.

He inserted the metal forceps down the line of the laryngoscope, their angled head and long arms allowing deep access. He grasped the nut with the round flat tips and pulled it out in one easy movement. Sophie burst into tears, running to her son's side.

'Why isn't he breathing yet, Daniel?' said Sophie, her relief short lived as Max lay deathly still.

'He will,' said Daniel confidently. 'How about I give him a little incentive?'

He quickly pinched his nephew's nose, took a deep breath and blew gently twice into the little mouth. Max took a breath and started to cough and then vomited and began to cry. Daniel felt a surge of relief almost overwhelm him.

Max's little lips and mottled skin pinked up almost instantly and Sophie picked him up and crushed her to him. She sobbed as she hugged her little boy for dear life. He cried in her arms, his fright and her hysteria upsetting him even more.

When the paramedics arrived a short time later they were pleased to see the crisis was over but put Max on some oxygen for a while anyway. It was purely for prophylaxis, given Max's brief spell of hypoxia.

Sophie couldn't believe the whole incident had lasted less than two minutes! It had seemed like an eternity when her son's life had hung in the balance and Daniel had brought him back from the brink.

The paramedics advised Sophie to transport Max to St Jude's so he could be monitored for a few hours but looking at him now, dancing to the music and giggling like the Max she knew and loved, Sophie declined. There was enough medical expertise in the house and should they be concerned about him they would get him there pronto.

Luckily the rest of the family backed her and the paramedics left, happy that they had discharged their duties. Everyone was still so relieved that Max was OK that they didn't want to let him out of their sight. They all just sat for a while and stared, watching him, drinking in his life and energy.

Sophie trembled whenever she thought about how close she had come to losing him. She sniffled and sucked in a deep breath. It hadn't happened. Max was OK. But the what ifs were never far away. She glanced at Daniel. What if he hadn't been there?

Max was nonplussed by all the fuss.

As Sophie tucked him into bed later she lectured him about nuts. He didn't look like he needed much convincing. Max had scared himself more than anyone and Sophie doubted he'd eat nuts ever again.

She watched him as he drifted to sleep, reluctant to leave his side. She lay beside him, snuggling his little body close to hers. Subconsciously Max reached for her hair and sucked his thumb. Sophie just lay there, inhaling his smell and counting her blessings. It had been a very scary day.

She woke an hour later with a kink in her neck and quietly crept out of his room. Sophie heard conversation drifting up from the lounge but didn't feel like company. She slipped out the back door and found herself heading for the wooden jetty where she had always gone to mull things over.

It was old and rickety but Sophie found the sound of the waves slapping the wood comforting and felt a strong connection with her childhood. She had fished and swum from this jetty. Skipped stones from it. Star-gazed from it on hot summer nights, lying on the rough boards, peering into the inky night sky. She'd even kissed Daniel on it.

The view from the end was as magnificent as always. A fairyland of lights on the opposite side of the river illuminated the CBD. She inhaled and the salty aroma filled her senses.

'You OK, Sophie?'

She didn't turn. She hadn't heard Daniel's approach but, then, she wasn't surprised by it either. If anyone had known where to find her after the events of the day, it would be Daniel.

She sensed rather than heard him come closer. The weathered boards always creaked underfoot but Daniel knew from years of sneaking up on her where to tread for maximum surprise. They had all known.

He sat beside her. He didn't say anything more and she was grateful for that. They just sat in companionable silence for a while. The magnitude of what could have happened was too horrific to speak about.

'Thank you, Daniel,' Sophie said, realising that she hadn't expressed her gratitude. 'I was so useless today. If you hadn't had been there... I don't know what came over me.'

'You're his mother, Sophie.'

'I'm a nurse—an emergency nurse—and I just went to pieces.'

'You're a mother first. I doubt I would have been any good either if it had been my child.'

Sophie closed her eyes as the tempo of her heartbeat increased. For the first time in a long time she didn't feel guilty about keeping the secret. She had needed Daniel today. To be the strong one, the one in control. Would he have been so calm if he had known that Max was really his son? Or would he have been as useless as her? Sophie suppressed a shudder.

They were quiet again for a while, only the lapping of the gentle tide and the sound of a passing boat interrupting their thoughts.

Daniel turned so he was facing her and not the view. 'What were you thinking about earlier today when Max was on my shoulders, before he decided to scare the hell out of us? You looked a little misty-eyed there for a moment.'

Sophie searched back through the jumbled haze that was her memory of the day. What had she been thinking about?

'I was thinking how Max had his father's eyes.' She turned to face him as well, their thighs almost touching. A very small space separated them.

'It's weird, isn't it? Not having Michael around? It just doesn't seem right somehow,' he said pensively.

'Nothing's been right since he died,' she said quietly.

She looked away as her mind drifted to that awful night two years ago. Michael had taken a tumble out of his wheelchair during the day, playing basketball, and had fractured his femur. She remembered how funny, how ironic he had thought it that a fracture, usually enormously painful, had been completely painless.

'Cheer up, babe.' He had laughed at her worried face. 'Just another advantage of being crippled.' And he had smiled to soften the words.

Later that night she'd had a phone call from St Jude's.

Michael had been rushed to ICU. The family had charged to the hospital but it had already been too late. They hadn't been able to revive him.

An autopsy later revealed what the doctors had suspected. A massive fat embolism, liberated from his bone marrow at the time of the fracture, had lodged in his pulmonary artery and sent him into cardiac arrest.

Daniel shifted beside her and called her back from the past. She turned to him again and they stared at each other for a short while.

'I'm sorry about last night. It was unforgivable.'

Sophie nodded. Yes. It had been. But that had been last night and tonight her son was sleeping in his bed soundly because Daniel had saved his life, and nothing else mattered next to that.

'I don't know what came over me, Soph,' he said huskily as she continued her silence.

Her arms prickled as goose-bumps broke out. He had called her Soph. Just like in the old days. She inhaled deeply to quell the mad stirrings in her body and the salty, earthy atmosphere took her further into her past.

'Sophie, please,' he begged.

She blinked at the ragged tone of his voice and snapped back to the present. 'Don't worry about it, Daniel,' she sighed. 'We both behaved unprofessionally. Let's leave it at that.'

'But—'

'Shh.' Sophie cut him off, placing her fingers against his lips. It was an impulsive move but in the circumstances seemed right.

She took her hand away. 'I just want to sit here and listen to the waves and be grateful that Max is alive. Can we do that?' she asked softly.

'Sure.'

They both turned back to face the view. After a while, Daniel lay back against the boards, his legs dangling over the edge. The waves and the insects were soothing, the breeze was balmy and the stars glistened like teardrops.

They sat for ages just as they had as children, absorbing the night. The years melted away. Max was alive. Their problems were insignificant.

CHAPTER FIVE

THE next morning at breakfast Sophie and Max were already eating when Daniel pushed John to the breakfast table.

'Morning, Maxy,' said John.

'Hello, G.G.,' said Max through a mouthful of corn-flakes.

'He doesn't seem to be suffering any adverse effects from yesterday,' John commented to Sophie as he held his cup out with his good arm for Sally to fill with coffee.

'No.' She shuddered. It made her feel sick whenever she thought about it. 'Thanks to Daniel.'

Daniel looked at her and she smiled at him and he smiled back. Something had happened last night out on the jetty. They hadn't discussed it—in fact, they'd barely spoken at all—but their relationship felt easier this morning. Free of some excess baggage.

'Yes,' John agreed, looking at his grandson. 'She's right, Danny, boy. You were brilliant. There may just be something to this paramedic nonsense after all.'

Sophie laughed. John had taken it hard when his favourite grandson had decided not to follow Monday family tradition. Under Arabella's roof alone there was a microbiology professor and a paediatric cardiologist, and Wendy was a geneticist. In fact, all the Mondays for generations had been involved in the medical profession. Even Michael had been studying to become a doctor when the car accident had crippled him.

Daniel had been the one exception. Nothing John had said had been able to dissuade him. There had been many heated exchanges. Diatribes about wasting his grades and his talents and how poor the pay was had had no effect. Daniel had stuck to his guns. More than that, he had excelled. Intensive Care Paramedic was a difficult status to achieve.

'Thanks, G.,' said Daniel, 'I'll take that as a compliment.'

'No, I mean it, Danny. I'm proud of you. I really am.'

Daniel stopped eating and put his knife and fork down. This was high praise indeed from John. He thought he saw a shimmer of tears in the old man's eyes and felt humbled. Disappointing his grandfather had always been one of his biggest regrets. 'I appreciate that, G. I really do.'

Sophie watched the exchange, feeling a little teary herself. Having been privy to a lot of the commotion that Daniel's decision had caused, she understood the magnitude of John's statement.

She knew Daniel had struggled about letting his grandfather down. In fact, at one stage he had felt so pressured that he had confided in her he was going to give in, give up his dreams and follow the Monday path.

'No!' She had been horrified. 'This is hard for you. You love John and don't want to disappoint him, but this is *your* life, Daniel. You have to do what's right for you.'

He had been eighteen then. And frankly, after yesterday, she had never been gladder that he had listened to a squirt of a kid, a twelve-year-old, and fulfilled his dream.

* * *

Life after Max's choking episode settled back to normal. Or as near normal as it could with John's rehabilitation dictating their days. His physical therapy became a family project.

Tina, the physio, was a tough taskmaster and just what a cantankerous old man needed. John was impatient with his weakness, wanting to move as quickly through his therapy as possible to a full recovery.

Tina knew he had to learn to crawl before he could walk and kept him on task with her persistence and iron will. John was stubborn but Tina was more so. She was also canny, involving everyone to keep her client on the straight and narrow.

Max loved 'helping' John and the little boy seemed to be the only one who could soothe John when his frustration got the better of him. Tina used Max to full advantage to bully John into just one more set of exercises.

The phone rang one morning after breakfast and Daniel picked it up. It was Tina.

'Something's come up and I can't make it today. I'd scheduled some hydrotherapy for John this morning. Are any of you free to do that with him? He was really looking forward to it. He knows the exercises.'

'I don't go on shift till tonight—I'll do it.'

'You may need a hand, getting him in and out,' she said, and rang off.

Daniel got changed into his swimmers and went looking for John. Martin, John's nurse, who came every morning for an hour, had helped his patient get ready for the pool. He handed the wheelchair over to Daniel and left as he was already running late for his next client.

Sophie and Max were in the water when they arrived.

The pool had been fully modified for Michael, who had swum every day, even in winter. It was fortuitous for John as it meant he could have regular hydrotherapy at home.

Daniel discarded his shirt and adjusted the waist draw-string on his boardies. A wet and smiling Sophie propelled herself out of the pool in one fluid movement, the water sluicing off her body like a waterfall. She sat on the edge and wrung the excess water out of her hair.

'Want a hand?' she called, keeping one eye on Max who was splashing around in the deep end, the yellow floaties attached to his upper arms keeping him above water.

She was wearing a bikini. A very tiny bikini. And it was the first time Daniel had seen her with so little on in a long time. Would it actually stay attached to her body if she helped?

Sophie walked towards him and he was struck by how her body had changed over the years. Her breasts seemed fuller, her hips slightly rounder. Her waist more obvious. She looked fantastic. The leanness of four years ago had been replaced by subtle curves—very womanly.

Maybe that was the difference. She was no longer a girl. She'd grown into a woman. She'd nurtured a baby in her womb, suckled him at her breast. She was a mother and had flowered accordingly. And he liked it! He liked it a lot.

She came close and between the three of them they got John into the pool. If there was one thing they both knew well, it was the manual handling of patients. Their jobs in-volved a lot of lifting and safe techniques were essential to prevent back injuries.

Sophie left them to it, joining Max at the other end of the pool. Daniel tried hard to concentrate on John's exercises. He knew water was an excellent medium to work on arm and leg strength—the exercise aided by the natural buoyancy. Still, the splashing and the giggling from the deep end was distracting.

'Why don't you go and join them?' said John.

'Hmm? What?' said Daniel.

'I'm perfectly capable of doing this myself, Danny, boy. The stroke didn't affect my intelligence.'

'Tina wouldn't approve of me shirking my responsibilities.'

'I won't tell her if you don't.'

'Unca Dan, Unca Dan.'

Daniel hesitated midway through manipulating John's arm through the water. He really didn't want to turn round.

'Go,' John insisted.

'Unca Da-a-an,' Max called again.

Daniel sighed as his grandfather winked at him. 'Stay close to the edge in case you lose your balance,' said Daniel.

'Aye, aye, Danny, boy.' John saluted him with his good arm.

Daniel rolled his eyes at his grandfather and pushed himself off the wall with his toes, swimming leisurely towards his insistent nephew. He ducked under the water as he approached and came up underneath Max, lifting him out of the water and tossing him. The floaties ensured he bobbed harmlessly in the water and the little boy squealed for more.

'He'll never tire of it,' warned Sophie, laughing at their antics.

She swam down to John, feeling a tad superfluous. Max

had taken to his Uncle Dan like a duck to water. He'd always been a boy who had identified with men. Max had grown up with several strong male role models and, apart from her and Sally and his grandmother, he much preferred male company.

He had adored Michael. His little face had lit up every time Michael had come into the room and, with him being a stay-at-home dad, they had formed a deep bond. If Sophie could find one positive aspect of Michael's death it was that, at two years of age, Max had been too young to fully understand. Just over two years later Max had no recall of the man who had been his father in every way that mattered.

Sophie watched John go through his exercises, helping him occasionally as he required. It was amazing how much he had improved in the last month. John's doctors and even Tina were certain he would always have a residual weakness due to the extent of the stroke, but John was determined to reduce the deficit to something only he was aware of.

John watched Sophie pretending to keep him company but not fooling him in the slightest. The squealing and laughter and splashing hadn't abated and he could read the wistful look in her eyes as easily as he had always been able to read her expressions.

'He'll make a great father,' John commented.

'Hmm,' said Sophie noncommittally, her eyes not leaving the other end. If only John knew the half of it!

'When are you going to tell Daniel he's Max's father?'

That got her attention! Her head snapped back to face him instantly.

'Wh-what?' said Sophie. John knew? But how?

'I'm not stupid, Sophie,' said John gently, to soften the blow.

'Stupid, no. Wrong, definitely.' Sophie gathered her wits. She hadn't kept Max's paternity a secret for four years to baulk the first time someone called her on it.

'You don't think I knew what was going on between you and Daniel just before the accident?'

'I don't know what you're talking about,' she spluttered turning her face away. She felt slightly dizzy from the rush of blood to her head.

'I know you thought you were being discreet but it was written all over both of your faces.'

'You're wrong, John,' she denied again. Her heart pounded. Had they been that obvious?

'I may be old but I know what young love looks like, my dear. You two had it bad.'

Sophie looked back at him again. She thought they'd hidden it so well. She didn't know what to say. It seemed pointless to continue to deny it when he so obviously knew what had happened. John's face told her the game was up. She should have been horrified, but perversely she wasn't. She was, what? Relieved?

John watched the play of emotions on her face and recognised the moment she surrendered. 'And then the accident happened and you and Michael announced your engagement and your pregnancy, and I put two and two together.'

'Why did you never say anything?' she asked quietly. The raucous noises from the deep end of the pool faded as she conceded. It was just her and John and this conversation. And the surprising lightening of a burden.

'Because for the first time in a month Michael was

happy. We'd been very worried about him. You know how terribly depressed he'd been and suddenly he was his old self again. You gave him a reason to live. You and Max. I didn't have the heart to mess with that, and I knew that Daniel and you had quarrelled and that you would love Michael just as you always had. I knew Michael needed you much more than Daniel. It makes me ashamed to admit it to you now but it seemed better to stay silent at the time.'

Sophie swallowed the lump rising in her throat. She could hear her heart pounding and was amazed to see that the water surrounding her wasn't vibrating in unison.

'Who else knows?' she asked quietly.

'Just me,' said John, 'although I suspect that Sally has an inkling. But we've never really spoken about it. Edward and Wendy were on the lecture circuit in Europe at the time of your affair and the accident, so they were unaware of what was happening.'

Sophie nodded, remembering that awful time. She'd come back to Arabella late at night after being out with some friends to find two policemen at the door talking to John. She'd never forget the dreadful feeling of foreboding that had settled in her gut.

'What?' she had said to John. One look at his stricken face had confirmed her worst fears. She had felt her legs buckle and one of the policemen had grabbed her around the waist as she had sagged against him.

They had charged up to St Jude's. The information had been sketchy. Just that both Daniel and Michael had been involved in a serious car accident and had been admitted to hospital, badly injured.

Sophie's overwhelming relief to find Daniel relatively unscathed had been tempered by Michael's critical status. It had been so hard to believe her dearest friend was lying so still and so close to death in St Jude's specialised spinal unit.

As the days had gone by and the three of them had maintained a bedside vigil, her relationship with Daniel had been put on hold. Edward and Wendy had rushed back from Europe just as Michael had improved enough to be out of Intensive Care. But with his paraplegia confirmed, Michael entered a dark depression.

He was alive, yes, but losing the use of his legs had been a major blow and his mood was difficult. But she went to see him every day, hoping by sheer force of will alone that she could make a difference to his life. She couldn't desert her best friend in his hour of need.

It was at the same time she discovered she was pregnant. It was the worst timing possible. The Monday family were dealing with enough, without putting this on their plate as well. What would Daniel think?

They'd seen each other rarely in the month since the accident and their time together was tempered with guilt. Guilt that they were both walking around, able to enjoy themselves, while the one other person who meant the world to both of them couldn't.

Daniel felt it most acutely. He had been driving the car and Sophie watched as guilt tore at his soul. It didn't matter that they had been struck by a car that had veered into their path from the other side of the road. It didn't matter that no one else blamed him for the accident, least of all Michael. His brother was crippled and that was all that mattered to Daniel. Injured in a car that he had been driving!

Daniel's self-reproach made him difficult to face about

her news. Sophie still hadn't told him when she burst into tears one morning in front of Michael, who had been particularly cantankerous and impatient. It had probably been the jolt Michael needed to jar him out of his self-pity. He certainly looked startled as he tried to comfort her and she blurted out her awful secret.

He was just like the old Michael, her dear, dear friend. He told her it would be OK and not to worry, and if Daniel didn't realise what a lucky man he was then he'd marry her and they'd bring up the baby together.

She laughed through her tears at his suggestion. But then Daniel rejected her love so callously later that night she found herself crying all over Michael again and he restated his proposal.

She dismissed the idea but when he explained how happy it would make him and she looked into his eager face, smiling for the first time in a month, she felt the strings of their longstanding friendship pull tight. It was the perfect solution.

'Michael made me promise I wouldn't tell,' she said quietly to John, coming back from the past.

'I can understand that,' said John, swishing his arms back and forth, using the natural resistance of the water. 'But he's dead now, Sophie. Do you think he meant you to take the secret to your grave?'

Had he? She didn't know any more. And just how did you have that kind of conversation anyway? 'It doesn't get any easier to tell him, you know?'

'Of course, my dear, of course. And whether you do or not makes no difference to me, but I think maybe he deserves to know. Look at him,' he said, nodding towards

Daniel frolicking merrily with his son. 'Look at Max. Maybe he also deserves a father?'

'He doesn't love me, John. We don't love each other.'

'And you and Michael did I suppose?'

He'd caught her out there. Michael had loved her. As a man. As a husband. Even though their marriage had been totally non-sexual, due to the level of Michael's paraplegia, he had never made any secret of the depth of his feelings for her. And he had understood her position. That she had loved him as a friend. A best friend. But that was all it would ever be for her.

'This is different, John.'

'Why? Because you still love him?'

'No,' she said. Because she didn't. Any love she may have felt for him once upon a time had died a painful death. 'Because it is. It just is.'

'Mummy!'

Max's excited yell interrupted the conversation.

Sophie and John turned to look at Max. He was standing on his uncle's shoulders, Daniel's big hands were holding Max by his thighs, steadying him. 'Watch me dive, Mummy.'

With that, he pushed off Daniel's shoulders like a little spring, holding both of his hands out in front of him with a diver's poise. He disappeared under the water briefly before the flotation devices on his arms bobbed him to the surface again.

Max beamed as his audience broke into spontaneous applause. 'That's definitely a ten, Maxy,' said John proudly.

Sophie caught Daniel's eye and they stared wordlessly at each other for a few moments.

'He's a chip off the old block,' said Daniel, as he held a squirming Max tightly in his arms.

Michael had been a champion diver at school. 'Yes,' said Sophie, burying herself even deeper in the lie. 'I guess he is.'

Sophie checked her watch. It was nine p.m. Only two hours to go until the late shift was over. Her feet ached from being on them for seven hours solid and she yawned as the familiar pool-induced tiredness she'd been fending off all day crept into her bones.

After splashing around for another hour, she and Max had got out of the pool. Max had fallen asleep as soon she had put him down for his midday nap. She'd known how he'd felt. The sun and the exercise had been conducive to sleep but Sophie had had to go to work and had resisted the temptation to lie down with her son.

The shift had been frantic and had helped to keep Sophie's mind off John's startling revelation. Two car accidents had kept them on their toes and despite their best efforts they had been unable to save two teenagers from dying.

It had been heavy going with the families and Sophie could still feel the chill down her spine as a mother's grief had reverberated around the walls of the department. It was like that sometimes. Some shifts just sucked.

It was always difficult to remain aloof from the tragedies that could occur here, and something they all struggled with but tonight held a particular element of reality for Sophie. It was hard not draw comparisons with Michael and Daniel's accident.

Michael had been left a paraplegic. Daniel had spent

every day since haunted by his guilt. But they had lived. And it took a night like tonight to really make her see how lucky they had been. Yes, Michael had suffered. But…what if they had both died?

How much more awful and tragic would it have been to lose her best friend and her lover in one dreadful blow? To have never seen Daniel's face again or talked to him or been near him. To have never had his son.

She closed her eyes, sickened by the notion, the cries of anguished mothers filtering through her disturbed thoughts. Just because she was over him, it didn't mean she wanted to live in a world where there was no Daniel.

It was with a heavy heart that she finally got the chance to take a teabreak. She didn't feel much like sitting alone in the tearoom so she sat down at the triage desk and started to load backlogged data onto the computer.

Looking at the stats, Sophie wasn't surprised to see that seventy-six patients had been triaged over the course of the shift. She took a sip of hot tea and glanced over to the empty waiting area—a most satisfying sight!

'Here she is,' said Todd, motioning to Leah. The two of them stood before her with silly grins.

'Hey, guys. What are you up to?' she asked, feeling the dullness leave her chest at the mischievousness in their eyes.

'Sophie Monday, may we present the Todd and Leah tap show,' said Todd in his very best radio DJ voice.

'What?' she asked, looking at them like they'd both escaped from the psych ward.

They laughed and began their routine, their work shoes clicking away on the hard linoleum of the department floor just like real tap shoes. Sophie laughed. How had they done that?

Todd hummed a tune and they tapped and leapt and pirouetted their way through an entire song. Sophie was laughing so hard as they built up to their grand finale she could hardly see. But thankfully she didn't miss the beautifully executed dip and the playful kiss Todd placed on his partner's lips.

'What exactly is going on here?' A shrill voice interrupted Sophie's clapping and Todd quickly pulled Leah to her feet.

'Ross,' said Sophie, sobering quickly and groaning inwardly. Not Ross, please. The after-hours nurse manager didn't have a humorous bone in his body.

'Doctor, I do not appreciate you leading my nursing staff astray. Sister Monday,' he went on, pointing his pencil at her, 'I expected more of you.'

'Ross, it's not as bad as it looks,' sighed Sophie. 'I was a bit down after what happened earlier and they were just trying to cheer me up.' Heaven forbid they should actually enjoy their work!

'I shouldn't have to lecture either of you on appropriate workplace behaviour.' His pencil jabbed the air again. Sophie looked behind Ross's head to see Leah pulling a funny face. She had to chew down on the inside of her cheek to stop herself from smiling.

'If you have nothing to do, I'm sure I could send you to another ward to help out.' With that he stuck his pencil behind his ear and turned on his heel, leaving them feeling like naughty schoolchildren.

They waited five seconds until they heard the squeaking of Ross's rubber soles fade away. And promptly burst out laughing. They laughed so hard they had to take it to the tearoom. Todd and Leah tippy-tapped in behind her.

'OK, what did you two do to your shoes?'

Leah bent her knee and flipped her foot up behind her, exposing the sole of her shoe. Two ECG dots, normally used when monitoring a patient's heart rhythm, were stuck to her shoes. They were round with a raised central metal nipple. And made a perfect tapping noise against the floor.

Sophie shook her head at the pair of them and laughed again. They each got a cup of tea and sat at the table.

'Is that guy for real or what?' asked Todd.

'Unfortunately, yes. Ross is a bureaucrat. He acts like every glove, syringe and bandage is paid for out of his own pocket. It's not important to like your job, just to do it well.'

'What's with that pencil? Where did it come from? He acts like he walks around with it shoved up his you know what!'

Sophie laughed at the image Todd had evoked.

'I would have thought something larger than the pencil.' Leah grinned and they laughed again. Oh, it was good to forget about their awful night.

'Speaking of which, I saw someone with a pineapple in his rectum a few years ago,' said Todd.

Leah and Sophie turned and looked at him with horrified expressions.

'True story,' he said, crossing his heart.

'Ouch,' said Leah.

'How did he do that?' asked Sophie.

'Slipped in the shower,' said Todd.

Sophie thought Leah was going to choke to death, she

was trying so hard to breathe and laugh at the same time. She slapped her on the back and they all had a quiet chuckle.

They were still there fifteen minutes later when Daniel strode into the room. Daniel had heard Sophie's familiar laugh from out in the hallway and noticed the slight kick of anticipation quicken his step. He had some paperwork to complete and needed a cup of coffee. Sophie's presence would be a bonus.

The first thing he saw was Todd touching Sophie on the shoulder. Something else kicked him this time. And it wasn't pleasant! He felt his stomach clench as the mere thought of Todd with Sophie did alarming things to his pulse rate. They didn't belong together. It was all wrong.

The second thing was that something was obviously highly amusing. All three of them looked like they'd been caught with their hands in the cookie jar. He noted the relief on their faces as they realised it was only him.

'Hello, Daniel,' Sophie said.

'Something funny?' he asked.

'Todd was just telling us about a patient with a foreign body in an awkward spot,' she said.

'That's one way of putting it, Soph. Seen any of those in your time, Daniel?' Todd asked.

Daniel watched as Todd kept his arm loosely around the back of Sophie's chair. Todd had called her Soph. Only he ever called her that. He felt his hackles rise. He didn't know why but…he just didn't like this guy. 'I've seen a few,' said Daniel quietly.

'Funny, isn't it?'

Sophie could tell from Daniel's face that he didn't find

it particularly amusing. His face looked closed, tense. He looked kind of angry and she really wasn't sure why.

'I've never found them to be particularly funny.'

Daniel's comment clanged like a loud bell around the room. Sophie shut her eyes and shook her head. Would it have killed him to have agreed? Was he going to make a scene now?

'O-O-K, then,' said Todd dropping his arms to his side and standing to go. 'Well…I have charts to tend to so I think I'll get going.'

Leah followed him quickly.

'What?' said Daniel, as Sophie glared at him.

'What the hell was that all about?' she demanded.

'I think laughing at a patient's expense is extremely poor form, don't you?'

'What?' she asked incredulously.

'Very unprofessional.'

She stared at him like he'd grown another head. Why was *he* acting like he had something shoved up his rectum? 'What?' she repeated.

Oh, damn! He sounded so pompous. Even to his own ears he sounded like a disapproving school teacher. He couldn't help himself—Todd irritated him big time! 'I mean, did the man not take the Hippocratic oath? And I don't think he needs any further encouragement from his groupies. Do you?' What was wrong with him? Why couldn't he just shut up?

'Groupies?' Was he implying that she was some simpering brainless fan?

'Yes, groupies. Is there something going on between you two? Because you're looking pretty damn cosy.'

Sophie's head was spinning. She was finding it hard to keep up. Her and Todd? Was he insane? Todd no more wanted to settle into a relationship than fly to the moon. And, besides, he was too…too…cute!

'And what if there is? What the hell's it got to do with you?' She was too angry to give him the satisfaction of a denial.

'You're right, it's got nothing to do with me. You just do whatever the hell you want. I keep forgetting that. I keep forgetting that you jump from man to man without a backward glance!'

Sophie felt sure her gasp could be heard all over the department. The unfairness of his comment stung. She heaved in some ragged breaths, two angry spots of colour staining her cheeks.

'How dare you?' she spat, dragging air into her lungs. 'How dare you come in here and accuse me of things and completely absolve yourself from any responsibility? Everything I've done you've driven me to, you sanctimonious bastard!'

Daniel immediately regretted his words. Too late. They were out now. He watched her as her dark blue eyes blazed in outrage. 'I'm sorry. OK? Hell, Sophie, I'm so sorry! That was unforgivable.'

She didn't look very mollified as she continued to glare daggers at him. 'I just think he has designs on you that you're maybe not aware of. Are you ready for that, Sophie? I mean, really ready?'

He had to be joking, right? He was so wrong about this it was almost laughable. 'Two things, Daniel. It's been two years since Michael died. I hardly think that constitutes jumping from man to man, do you? Secondly,' she went on, not wanting or caring for him to answer, 'you have no idea what we've been through tonight. I've watched a seventeen- and an eighteen-year-old die. I've comforted their fathers and I've held their mothers. I'm sorry that we seemed a little callous to you, but we *really* needed to laugh about something.'

Daniel shut his eyes. He'd stuffed up—big time. He knew that sometimes you had to laugh or you'd cry. Was sorry going to cut it? It seemed inadequate. 'Soph, I'm so sorry. I don't know what came over me.'

'Frankly, Daniel, I don't really care. I didn't think you could possibly hurt me any more than you already have over the years. Guess I was wrong about that.'

And with as much dignity as she could muster, she brushed past him without a backward glance.

CHAPTER SIX

SOPHIE'S legs shook all the way to her car. Daniel's accusations had hurt. She heaved in a breath and closed her eyes hard to stop the tears that were threatening. She'd cried too many tears over Daniel Monday.

But the tears were easier to stop than the memories, and as she drove to Arabella they crashed all around her and flooded her with their smells and voices. Michael's funeral replayed in her head, the grief and sorrow still there two years on.

The heady smell of roses that Charlie had cultivated over the years and picked from Arabella's rose garden to place on the coffin. The poignant notes of the flute that had played as Michael had been committed to the ground. The smell of the rain hitting the earth as the drizzly weather had mirrored the sombre mood.

The utter misery of Wendy's sobs as she'd thrown soil into the hole in the ground and Max's confusion as he had grizzled and clung to her, too young to understand but canny enough to know something really awful had happened.

People had been so kind. Marquees had been erected in Arabella's gardens and everyone had made a special effort to seek her out and express their deepest sympathies. Even Daniel's presence hadn't managed to pierce the bubble of grief that had encapsulated her. Her husband, her best friend was dead. Michael…

Later that night Max had taken for ever to go to sleep. He had cried for his daddy and she had lain with him, hugging his little body close, their tears mingling. She had rocked him gently and crooned 'Beautiful boy' to him, just as Michael had done every night of Max's life. Finally they had both fallen into an exhausted sleep.

Sophie woke a few hours later taking a few seconds before she orientated herself and the unrelenting grief settled around her again. She got up carefully and didn't know what to do with herself. She couldn't face going to bed. Lying alone in the king-sized bed was too painful to think about.

She wandered around the house for a bit, finally coming to the formal lounge. She moved to the bay window and absently fingered one of the two comfy, over-stuffed chairs that faced each other. A low coffee-table that held the chessboard separated the two.

This room held so many memories. This was where John had taught the three of them to play chess. Michael hadn't been overly interested but Daniel had and so, therefore, had she. The hours they had spent, the games they had played, sitting on these chairs.

A noise from behind disturbed her and she turned to discover Daniel standing in the doorway.

'Sophie,' he said in a voice that echoed her misery and grief.

She didn't answer him. Just turned back to cast her unseeing gaze to the river view. She heard him approach and could feel her body tremble with a build-up of emotion.

'I'm so sorry, Soph,' he whispered, and placed his hands on her shoulders.

And it was her total undoing. She crumpled. Days of putting on a brave face and being strong for Max disintegrated in an instant. She turned in his arms and he pulled her tight into his chest and she let it all flow out.

If there was one person in this world who understood how she felt, it was Daniel. For so many years they had been like the Three Musketeers. Inseparable. Her memories of Michael were so joined with those of Daniel that it was hard to separate them. She knew he was grieving every bit as much as her.

He held her and whispered his sorrow and kissed her forehead and her cheeks, as he had always done when she had hurt herself as a child. It was comforting and seemed so right, so natural. And then she stopped crying and just stood in the circle of his arms, listening to his heartbeat.

She wasn't sure when it changed, if there had been a moment or a nuance when she had become aware of his body on a physical level. But suddenly it felt different. Like he was holding her differently or his breathing had changed.

And then she became aware of his hardness. The events unfolded as if in slow motion. His obvious arousal, the thudding of his heart against her ear, the sudden stiff-armed, robot-like way he held her. Kind of awkward, like he was trying to create some space between them.

She looked into his eyes and even in the gloom she could see the flash of desire that dilated his pupils and took her back to the days when they had been lovers.

'Sophie,' he said again, and his voice was full of aching and need and want, and he was so close and smelt so good and felt so wonderful.

And then they were kissing. Flashpoint had been reached and they exploded. Sophie couldn't get enough of him. He tasted just like she remembered. Kissed just like she remembered. And she hadn't been kissed in the longest time.

Sure, Michael had kissed her but their marriage had never been consummated. After many frustrating attempts they had let the idea go. Michael had said if he couldn't have it all then he didn't want anything, and she had been more than happy to agree.

They'd shared a bed and been as close physically as was possible for two people who weren't having sex. She'd never had sexual feelings for him anyway and apart from the odd frustrated episode she'd put all those emotions on ice.

But Daniel had melted them away with one kiss and she was so hungry for more she was frightened she'd die of starvation before she could be sated.

The inevitable happened. They gave no thought to the consequences or the guilt that would follow. All they could think and feel was the moment and the wonderful sensation of coming home.

It took about a minute after they'd made love for the realisation to kick in.

'Oh, God. What have we done?' Daniel sat up, pushing himself away from her, disgust at his actions in every line of his semi-naked body.

She didn't answer and he turned back to look at her. She remembered flinching as his eyes, full of disgust, had flicked over her. Her blouse had been yanked open, her bra pushed aside, her skirt had ridden up around her waist.

He had stood, straightening his clothes as she'd lain there, still trying to work out what had happened. 'For heaven's sake, Sophie, fix yourself up,' he had snapped.

She had got up from the floor feeling sullied and used. He'd refused to look at her and she hadn't understood why he'd seemed to think it had been her fault. 'Daniel?' she said, her voice small.

He ignored her. 'What were we thinking?' he asked, turning to her, his eyes beseeching her, looking for an answer she didn't have.

They hadn't been thinking. It had just happened. A reaction to their grief and loss at a time when they were both seeking comfort. It hadn't made it right. It hadn't made it any easier to swallow. But it was what it was.

'Why did you let me do that?' he demanded.

'Daniel—'

'We just put your husband in the ground a few hours ago. How could you do this to him?'

Sophie knew that Daniel was struggling with what had happened, struggling with his own guilt, but his words stung and she remembered the deafeningly sound of her slap as it connected with his cheek. 'My husband. Your brother. How could *you*, Daniel? How could you?'

She walked out on him then and Daniel went back to New York a couple of days later. They hadn't talked about it then and had only skirted around it the other night. As Sophie parked her car she acknowledged it was still there between them. Still a thorn in their sides.

* * *

'Unit 001, thirty-year-old male. GSW to left femur. Is conscious and breathing but leg is apparently haemorrhaging significantly. Injury followed a bungled bank robbery. Assailants have left the scene and police are present. Being backed up by unit 912.'

'Roger, Coms.'

Daniel hung up the radio and sped, lights and sirens blazing, to the address in Fortitude Valley given to him by the communications centre. Years of living in New York had fostered a certain nonchalance concerning gunshot wounds. He'd seen hundreds of them! Rarely would a day go by on the job when he hadn't dealt with at least one.

So, consequently, his mind wasn't full of possible scenarios and clinical issues. It was full of Sophie. He hadn't slept a wink the last couple of nights, thinking about what had transpired between them. He pushed those thoughts aside and tapped into the hum of adrenaline running through his system and channelled it to sharpen his mind and prepare his body.

He reached the scene fairly quickly. The experience of years of being a paramedic came to the fore as he climbed out of his vehicle. Someone had been shot and needed him. Everything else took a back seat.

There was chaos at the scene as Daniel approached. Four police cars blocked the road. The victim had been shot on the footpath outside the bank and a crowd of curious onlookers, being held at bay by the police, was adding to the noise.

The man was clutching his bloodied leg and groaning in agony. A large pool of blood was congealing on the cement. Another bank employee was trying to apply pressure but quite ineffectually as the victim kept rolling around.

Daniel's mind was in purely clinical mode as he drew nearer. D for danger. Police were present and the bad guys had fled. Check.

R for response. Patient was groaning and swearing about the pain. Normal response. Check.

A for airway. The man appeared to have a perfectly patent airway if the swear words were any indication. Check.

B for breathing. Well, it was a bit hard to swear if you couldn't breathe. Check.

C for circulation. Again, swearing was exceedingly difficult to achieve if you were pulseless. Check.

H for haemorrhage. Bingo! 'Hey, mate,' said Daniel, snapping on some gloves and pulling a sterile dressing pad out of his kit. The assistant gratefully gave up his spot so Daniel had room to work. 'I'm Daniel. I'm a paramedic. What's your name?'

Daniel eased the makeshift dressing away from the wound gently so he could assess the damage, not wanting to disturb any clot that may have formed. The injury was in mid-thigh. Not pumping and the blood seemed darker and therefore venous. That was good but it was still oozing considerably. Taking a rough guess at his patient's blood loss, Daniel thought he'd probably lost close to a litre.

'Gordon,' he groaned. 'He shot me. I can't believe he bloody shot me!'

'Are you hurt anywhere else?' asked Daniel as he replaced the pad with a sterile one and bandaged it firmly in place, exerting more pressure over the top with his hand. He did a quick visual head-to-toe check.

The man shook his head vigorously. 'It's just me bloody leg!'

'Right, you,' said Daniel, pointing to the person who had been helping when Daniel had arrived. He'd introduced himself as Reg. 'You were doing a great job, Reg. You reckon you can hold this for me again? Firm pressure, OK?'

His helper did as he was asked but their patient continued to roll around a bit.

'Gordon, you need to keep still so we can apply effective pressure.'

'Hurts too bloody much to stay still,' he yelled, and groaned again.

Daniel heard his back-up arrive. 'I'm going to put you on oxygen and then put in a drip. We'll be able to give you some pain relief then. OK?'

'Whatever, mate! Just do it,' he snapped.

The back-up paramedics joined the scene and Daniel quickly allocated them jobs. Being an IC para, Daniel had seniority and controlled the scene. As he inserted the IV, Gordon was being hooked up to a monitor and having his vital signs recorded.

'BP ninety systolic.'

Daniel assessed the information. It wasn't too low but for a man in extreme pain you'd have expected it to be higher, unless he'd lost a large amount of circulating blood volume. Hypovolaemic shock was to be avoided at all costs.

Daniel hooked up a plasma supplement and ran it in as fast as it would go to replace the blood loss. He also administered a dose of morphine and Gordon became easier to manage.

Daniel's next concern was whether Gordon's femur was

fractured. That could be causing a large part of Gordon's pain. Daniel suspected it had been, and guessed it had probably splintered into many shards if it had taken the full force of the bullet.

If he could splint the leg, using a figure-of-eight technique applied to Gordon's feet, he would be able to apply traction to his injured leg and hopefully reduce his pain further. Daniel didn't want to move him until they'd stabilised his femur.

Working as a team, the three paramedics quickly and efficiently applied the figure-of-eight bandage and then splinted both legs together. Daniel was satisfied they could load Gordon now his haemorrhage was being efficiently controlled, his fracture reduced and his lost fluids were being replaced.

Daniel drove to the hospital behind the ambulance. His patient was as stabilised as he could be in a pre-hospital setting, so he found his thoughts returning to Sophie. He knew she was working today. What were the chances they would meet?

Very good actually. Sophie's face was the first he saw as he entered St Jude's. He stared at her and saw her momentary surprise.

'Sophie.'

'Daniel.' Her tone was brisk. Her actions methodical. 'What have we got here?' she asked, refusing to look him in the eye.

Daniel sighed and handed his patient over to her with the most professional façade he could muster. If she could pretend nothing had happened, so could he. He fought the urge to stick around, guessing it would make her job a lot easier without him hovering in the background. Gordon was in good hands and he had definitely been dismissed!

The silent treatment continued at Arabella. Thank goodness for Max. At least he didn't treat him like a pariah. Not that he didn't deserve it. Daniel knew he had been way out of line the other night. He had tried to talk to Sophie about it a couple of times but she was obviously still pretty angry with him.

'What did you do to my mummy?' Max asked him one morning after Sophie had left the breakfast table the minute Daniel had arrived—again.

'What makes you think I did something?' asked Daniel, amused by the observation skills of his three-year-old nephew. It must be fairly obvious if Max had noticed!

'She does that dippy thing with her eyebrows when she looks at you,' he said, stuffing some toast into his mouth. 'Like she does at me when I've been naughty.' Max did a fairly good impression of his mother's frown.

'Oh,' said Daniel, chuckling. Out of the mouths of babes... 'I said something to upset Mummy. Something I shouldn't have said.'

'Don't worry, Unca Dan,' said Max, patting Daniel on the hand. 'Mummy never stays angry for long.'

Oh? The way he figured it she'd been angry at him for longer than Max had been on the planet. He looked down at his nephew's hand on his and felt a little pang in his gut. Oh, to be so innocent, so trusting! Sophie had done a great job. Michael, too. The pang intensified. How lucky his brother had been.

In many ways he hadn't, of course. He'd been a paraplegic and had died too young, but he'd also had Sophie and sired a son. Surely, in the grand scheme of things, those were the things that mattered?

Looking down at the little hand, he found himself absurdly jealous of his brother. And something else. Determination crystallised in his mind. Determination to be a part of this little boy's life, maybe pick up where his brother had been so cruelly torn away.

He suddenly regretted the last two years he had wasted on the other side of the world. Max needed him. As a role model, a father figure, even as a link to Michael. What was that old saying? It took a whole village to raise a good child. He knew with sudden clarity as the little hand warmed his that he wanted to be a big part of his nephew's life.

Daniel hung onto the side of his seat as the ambulance flew through the streets of Brisbane. The first rays of daylight streaked the sky. He was in the back with Beryl and she was in serious trouble. He could hear the screaming sirens from the inside and hoped they'd make it in time. If she stopped breathing and they had to pull over so he could intubate her, the outlook would be extremely grim.

'What's our ETA?' Daniel called to Adam, the student paramedic, who, despite his inexperience, was driving like a rally car professional. Beryl's husband, Fred, was in front beside Adam.

'Two minutes.'

'Radio Coms to update St Jude's on our ETA. Let them know she's developing ST elevation.' Daniel put on his best clinical voice so as not to alarm Fred, but the changes to Beryl's heart rhythm were worrying.

Beryl was sitting upright on the trolley, hanging onto the rails for stability as the ambulance swayed from side to side. She reminded him of a frog—large frightened eyes practically bulging out of her head, leaning as far forward as she could get, her neck outstretched and gulping in the oxygen through the mask like a frog catching flies. The effort to breathe was so severe she couldn't even manage the occasional word.

'Beryl, have you got any chest pain?' he asked, touching her sweaty arm.

She nodded, unable to talk. He looked at her blood-pressure reading on the monitor and decided it could handle a shot of glyceryl trinitrate. If, as he suspected, she was developing cardiac ischaemia due to hypoxia then a quick spray of the drug under her tongue should dilate the coronary arteries and improve the blood flow to the heart muscle itself.

An infarction of her cardiac tissue would indeed be a very bad complication and anything he could do to avert such an event was essential. He administered one spray underneath her tongue with barely a disruption to her oxygenation.

The vehicle swung into St Jude's ambulance bay shortly after that and Daniel didn't wait to be let out. He opened the doors from the inside and had the trolley half out by the time Adam joined him.

'Let's hustle,' he said, his jaw set in a grim line as they rushed the trolley inside.

The team met them on their way in and rushed the trolley through to the resus bay. Sophie was there and Daniel nodded silently as he helped the team move Beryl quickly and efficiently from his stretcher to their trolley.

'Acute exacerbation of COAD. Administered bronchodilators and IV steroids on scene with no noticeable improvement. Poor bilateral air entry. Developed ST elevation in the last two minutes. One dose of GTN given.'

Sophie listened to Daniel's concise handover as she hooked her patient up to the monitor. She looked at him and saw his blue eyes convey the things that he hadn't said. He was worried. Really worried.

A quick assessment of Beryl had her agreeing. It was the worst she had ever seen the elderly woman. She was cold, pale and clammy and gulping in air as fast as she could. Her body was desperately trying to get as much oxygen as possible. If that meant snatching the next breath before the last one had finished then so be it. She can't go on like this, Sophie thought.

'She's going to arrest,' said Daniel softly, standing behind her.

Sophie nodded. Beryl certainly couldn't keep this up for much longer. She moved closer to Beryl and covered her hand with her own.

'Please, Beryl. Try and slow your breathing down.' Sophie smiled and spoke in a confident manner. The last thing she wanted to do was panic Beryl by allowing her alarm to colour her voice.

The old woman clutched Beryl's hand and she noted the iciness. 'I know you're scared but you're here now. Let us take care of you.'

'H…h…' Beryl stuttered in a fragile whisper.

Sophie brought her head closer to try and catch what her patient was saying.

'Help.'

Then suddenly, just as Daniel had predicted, Beryl stopped breathing. Her eyes rolled back and she lost consciousness. Daniel was paged away to another call as the team sprang into action. He left reluctantly, sure that Beryl would not make it through this episode, and he worried how Sophie would cope.

Sophie didn't even notice his departure as dread settled in the pit of her stomach. Beryl! No. Don't do this to us, please. Sophie's thoughts were frantic as she quickly laid the back of the bed flat. For a few minutes as they bagged oxygen into her lungs via a resus mask, her heart trace on the monitor continued. But Sophie watched in dismay as it slowed and the ST elevation returned, indicating major cardiac involvement.

Sophie remembered the heart enlargement on the last chest X-ray Beryl had had. It was a common side effect of chronic airway disease. Years of lung dysfunction eventually put a strain on the heart. The heart grew larger, trying to compensate, and eventually it became too stretched and baggy to work effectively.

Thanks to the two IV lines Daniel had placed on scene, they were able to give drugs to speed up her heart rate and support her blood pressure.

'I'm in,' said Todd.

Sophie attached the black bag to the end of the endotracheal tube Todd had placed in Beryl's throat to allow them to ventilate Beryl's lungs. She met immediate resistance to her attempts to push air into the lungs.

'Her lungs are incredibly stiff,' she stated, her brow puckering in concentration. 'I can hardly ventilate them at all.'

'She's in VF,' said Richard as the monitor blared a warning at them. He started chest compressions.

'Charging the defib,' said Karen as she slapped two self-adhesive pads on Beryl's bare chest. The machine pinged its readiness. 'All clear,' Karen said in a firm, loud voice.

Sophie dropped the bag and stepped back. Everyone stopped what they were doing and did the same. Karen pushed the shock button and delivered the current.

'Still VF,' said Todd as they all resumed their places. 'Charge to 360,' he said, listening to Beryl's chest with a stethoscope. 'She's not shifting any air at all,' he confirmed with Sophie. 'Her lungs have had it.'

Years of chronic airway disease had made Beryl's lungs difficult to oxygenate adequately. During an acute episode such as this, the airways constricted right down, making it almost impossible to push air into them. Beryl's lungs had come to the end of the road.

The team worked on her for another fifteen minutes but when they couldn't ventilate her or restart her heart it became obvious it was futile. They stopped the resuscitation, Todd declaring Beryl's life extinct.

'I'd say she had significant cardiac infarction by the look of those ST segments,' Todd said.

Sophie agreed. Beryl's lungs were bad enough. Her heart failing also had made it a lethal combination. And it had only ever been a matter of time while she had continued to smoke. Sophie knew that. But that didn't make it any less sad.

In fact, it probably made it harder. Knowing Beryl could have avoided dying in such a way just highlighted the absolute waste. It was always sad when a favourite patient passed away and more so when their death could have been prevented.

Half an hour later Sophie was startled by the harsh clatter of the curtain being pulled back.

'Hi,' said Leah.

Sophie was surprised that the time had got away from her and the morning shift had arrived. She had gathered everything she needed and prepared to make Beryl presentable for Fred.

'Off home for you,' Leah said, feigning a stern voice. 'You've had an awful night. No one expects you to do this.'

'No,' said Sophie, smiling gently at her friend. 'I can't leave her like this. I promised her hubby I'd see to her and anyway…I think I need to do it for me as well.'

'I'll help.'

'No,' Sophie said firmly. 'It won't take long. I'll yell when I need a hand.'

Sophie was grateful that Leah had been around long enough to understand that there were some things you had to do by yourself. Laying someone out was never a great job but if you were particularly fond of a patient it was the final respectful thing you could do for them. It was an honour and a privilege and Sophie didn't know one nurse who didn't treat the often sad job with the utmost reverence.

Sophie talked quietly to Beryl as she gently washed the old lady's wrinkled, papery skin. She removed the endotracheal tube and the IV cannulas. She chatted about the time they had first met when Sophie had been a student nurse.

Leah gave her a hand to change the sheets and put a clean hospital gown on Beryl. Sophie combed Beryl's thin grey hair as Leah went to find Fred. She pulled a chair up close to the trolley so Fred could sit with her as long as he liked.

He entered a few moments later, looking older than his

eighty-odd years, and sat in the chair. Sophie felt her eyes well with tears as Fred took his wife's hand and a sob choked in his throat.

'What am I going to do without you, my girl?' he asked her. He laid his head on the bed beside her and placed her hand against his cheek.

Sophie left quietly, not wanting to intrude on such an intimate moment. It was humbling to witness and Sophie had to remind herself that some people stayed together for a lifetime. That their love for each other at the end of their lives had grown and magnified into something beautiful and ageless.

Sophie left work an hour late that morning but didn't mind. Tending to Beryl and chatting with Fred for a while had been very rewarding. He had thanked her for making Beryl look as beautiful as the day he had met her and Sophie had blinked rapidly to dispel the tears that had pricked at her eyes.

He obviously hadn't seen the external ravages of age or chronic disease that Sophie had seen when she'd looked at Beryl. His love and devotion had blinded him to such details. He had seen only the girl he had once known.

Sophie wondered if she'd ever have anyone in her life who would love her that much.

CHAPTER SEVEN

JOHN was an astute old goat, thought Sophie as she headed for the beach house. His suggestion that she get away overnight by herself had been a good one. Beryl's death had affected her more than she had realized, and with all the recent upheaval it was just one more thing she hadn't needed.

Sally had urged her as well, insisting that Max would be treated like a king and spoilt rotten until her return. When she had pointed out that that wasn't exactly what Max needed, Sally had shooed her away and gathered her surrogate grandchild to her ample bosom.

Max had squealed in delight and Sophie had felt a niggle of jealousy. It had looked pretty comforting there in Sally's arms and for the first time in a long time she found herself missing her mother.

Not that her mother had had the capacity to nurture and love that screamed from every cell of Sally's body. No, she had always been much too fragile for that. But there was the odd memory of being held tight and feeling totally loved. And it was that that Sophie chose to hold dear.

Sophie heard the crash of waves as she opened the door

of her Beetle and the sea breeze lifted her caramel hair off her neck. She looked at the big old bungalow with its wide wrap-around verandah facing the ocean and felt the cloud lift a little.

The water beckoned. She parked her car in the garage and stripped off her clothes to reveal the bikini beneath. She left her overnight bag by the front door and set off for the ten-minute walk down to the sand. She would open up after she'd had her fix of sand and sea.

The water was cool on her hot skin and Sophie dived eagerly into the waves. The ocean was just the right medicine for a hot day and a preoccupied mind. It was hard to think of anything other than one's place in the cosmos as the rhythm of the waves, as old as time, surged around your body.

Half an hour later Sophie walked out of the ocean and towelled off. The temptation to lie in the sun for a while almost won out, but her common sense overrode it.

She would, no doubt, fall asleep lulled by the rhythmic slapping of the waves against the shoreline and the drugging caress of the UV rays. She'd wake up two hours later burnt to a crisp even though it was getting past the hottest part of the day.

She walked a little further up the beach where the tree-line met the sand and sat in the shade. She donned her sunglasses and absorbed the natural beauty, feeling her tensions ease as each wave hit the beach.

Sally and John were chatting in the kitchen when Daniel entered, looking for something to eat. Sally fixed him a sandwich.

'I was thinking I might go to the beach house tonight.

I've got a couple of days off now and I can hear the ocean calling my name.'

Sally and John looked at each other. 'That's a good idea,' said Sally. 'There's nothing like a bit of salt air to clear the head.'

John looked at her, a small smile on his face. Just as he had always suspected—Sally knew more than she let on! 'I agree,' said John, still looking at their mischievous housekeeper. 'That's a good idea, Danny, boy.'

Sally turned away and busied herself at the sink but not before John caught her widening smile and the speculative glint in her eyes.

'I'd better go and pack, then,' Daniel said, putting his plate in the dishwasher. 'Where's Max? I'll just say good-bye to him.'

'He's asleep,' said Sally, turning back quickly to face Daniel. It was the truth, but the last thing she needed was for Daniel to hang around waiting for Max to wake up. She loved that child like her own but, as dear as he was, she knew he was a blabbermouth. 'I'll tell him.'

John and Sally's collective sigh when Daniel finally left was audible all over Arabella.

'So,' said John, amusement lighting his eyes, 'playing Cupid, Sally Jones?'

'You know as well as I, John Monday, that those two belong together and always have, and if Michael hadn't been paralysed they'd be married by now with maybe an-other Max or two.' She said it sternly but spoilt it totally by grinning a moment after her little speech had ended.

'Sally Jones, you old fox.' He'd always had an inkling that the ever-present housekeeper knew more than she let on.

'I'd be careful who I was calling old, John Monday,' she sniffed, and gave him a wink as she turned back to the sink.

The walk back up the hill was much more taxing, and Sophie was glad to have reached the top. She stopped and washed off the sand at the outdoor shower, before making her way to the front door and inserting the key.

She was really tired now, the exercise and the sun and the salt air combining with her paltry sleep that morning to eradicate thoughts of anything other than bed.

She headed straight for the bedroom she usually occupied, switched on the air-conditioner and fell onto the bed, still in her bikini. Not Beryl's death, not Max, not John, not even Daniel, who had occupied too much of her head space lately, intruded on her deep, dreamless sleep.

When Daniel pulled up a little while later he, too, felt the pull of the ocean and went for a swim before he did anything else. When he finally entered the house the shadows were lengthening, although there was still probably a couple of hours of daylight left.

He could smell the stuffiness caused by the house having been locked up for so long and methodically went through the entire place, opening all the windows so air could circulate. One of the guest bedrooms' doors was closed and he thought how odd that was when all the others weren't. He pushed it open and stopped dead.

Sophie was startled from her sleep, sitting bolt upright as the noise of the door being opened knifed through her.

'Daniel? You scared the daylights out of me,' she said as her heart pounded frantically in her chest.

'Sorry…I didn't know you were here.' And that you would be wearing next to nothing.

'Hmm.' She yawned, lying back down and shutting her eyes, the pull of slumber beckoning her back to its enticing embrace. His presence didn't really register she was so tired!

Daniel tried not to stare at her barely covered body. It was hardly an itsy-bitsy bikini by any stretch of the imagination. Boy-leg chocolate brown bottom and a crop-top style matching bra. His eyes were drawn to a delicate silver chain adorning her neck. A butterfly with mother-of-pearl wings hung from the chain fluttering at her cleavage.

He shut the door and shook his head to clear it, trying not to think about her bare skin and curves. She was here, too. Maybe he should leave? By the look of her not-quite-awake eyes he doubted she'd even remember he had been here. But it seemed so ridiculous to drive two hours just for a swim. Surely they were both adult enough to get along for one night?

Actually, the more he thought about it the more confident he became. He owed her an apology and she hadn't really given him the chance to do so. Alone with him tonight, she wouldn't really have a choice. He would cook for her, his very best cuisine. A special, please-forgive-me, apology dinner. He grabbed his car keys and went out for supplies.

The room was dark when Sophie finally woke up. She jumped in the *en suite* shower and dressed in a denim miniskirt and a purple V-necked T-shirt. She opened the bedroom door and the most delicious aroma tickled her senses. The image of Daniel bursting into her room came abruptly back to her. Maybe it hadn't been a dream. Maybe he really was here, too.

But why? Surely he had told John or someone at the house his plans? And surely they had told him she was already here? Had he followed her here for a reason? Did he want to thrash things out with her again? Revisit their awful argument and try and explain himself?

Sophie shook her head. Things had been awkward since their row, sure, but Beryl's death had made their angry words insignificant. They were both alive. That was something to be grateful for. It was just another argument, one of many they'd had and probably, knowing them, just one of many still to come.

She made her way through the house and leaned against the archway that led into the kitchen and beyond to the open-plan dining and lounge room and eventually to the massive deck overlooking the ocean.

Daniel was humming to himself as he cooked. He was chopping something on the chopping board, his back to her, and she took a moment to just stare. He was dressed in denim shorts and a white T-shirt, looking very casual and comfortable in such a domestic scene. A man who was comfortable with cooking—what woman could resist that?

He turned to get something from the fridge and spotted her.

'Hi,' he said hesitantly. 'I'm making us some tea. I hope you don't mind?'

'What are you doing here, Daniel?' she sighed. 'I'm really not in the mood to go round and round the houses with you tonight.'

'I know, I'm sorry, I didn't know you were here. John

didn't mention it when I told him I was coming. I wouldn't have come if I'd had known, Sophie.'

Sophie accepted Daniel's words at face value. She had a sneaking suspicion the old man was trying to pull their strings. Did John expect her to blurt out the truth simply because they were alone? Didn't he realise how difficult it was for her?

'Look, you've had a tough day and, whether we like it or not, we're both here. Let's just make the best of it. I made you a tropical cocktail.' He plonked it in her hand. 'Go outside and drink it. Tea is half an hour away.'

She didn't argue with him. The sight of him cooking dinner seemed too cosy, too appealing, so getting as far away as possible seemed like a most sensible suggestion. She wandered out to the deck and noticed that he'd turned the fairy lights on so she walked down the steps to the garden and made her way to the love seat.

She sipped at her drink, its fruity taste and the crushed ice very pleasant on this balmy night. The house looked magnificent and Sophie knew that from its elevated position the lights could be seen from miles around. Max would love them when the whole family came up next week for the annual pilgrimage to celebrate his birthday.

She watched as Daniel walked towards her, a drink in his hand.

'Do you mind if I join you?' he asked.

She shuffled over and they swung together silently for a few minutes as his weight caused the love seat to rock.

'So…Beryl…' he said gently.

'Died.'

'Yes. I rang St Jude's. I'm so sorry, Sophie. I know she was a favourite of yours.'

'*Que sera sera*,' she said, and smiled sadly.

'I—'

'Please, Daniel,' she interrupted, 'don't spoil the moment with I told-you-sos.'

'I wasn't going to, Soph, I'm not totally without tact! I was just going to say that it seemed like such a waste of a life.'

'Yes,' she said quietly, 'it was.'

They sat, not speaking, absorbing the night atmosphere. They could hear the waves crashing on the beach below, the insects humming raucously, and the vision of the fairy lights completed the magic.

Daniel finished his drink. 'Come on, dinner is served,' he said, and walked into the house with Sophie trailing behind.

She sat at the beautifully set table and whistled. 'Did you invite the Queen?' She smiled. 'What's this all about, then?'

'It's my way of apologising,' he said as he served up their food. 'I was totally out of line the other night. I don't know what came over me. It was unforgivable.'

'You're right, it was, but lucky for you I'm a very forgiving person.'

'That's sounds promising,' he said as he placed a glass of wine in front of her.

'It's amazing how very little it seems to matter now. John's stroke, Max's choking episode, Beryl…things like that put petty differences into perspective.'

'Amen,' he said, and clinked his glass with hers.

Their meal got under way and Daniel was grateful he could occupy himself with something other than looking at Sophie. The damn butterfly necklace was most distracting, his eyes drawn to it over and over again.

Cooking was one of his passions and with Sally's tutoring, as well as living alone for years, his culinary skills had been well and truly honed. He had skipped the idea of keeping it simple and had cooked to impress. It was only what Sophie deserved after what he had accused her of.

And when Sophie bit into the superbly cooked beef Wellington and shut her eyes and sighed blissfully, well…it was the greatest compliment. Some tiny pieces of flaky pastry stuck to her lips before she licked them away and Daniel stared, helpless to stop.

They talked. Actually talked, just like the old days. He'd forgotten how much they'd once laughed together. They stuck to safe subjects—work, Max, John and Max's upcoming birthday. And Daniel relaxed and actually enjoyed himself.

Daniel served the dessert—a melt-in-the-mouth chocolate mousse—and then they moved to the lounge for coffee.

'Port?' Daniel asked as he placed her mug on the coffee-table along with a plate of colourfully wrapped chocolate mints.

'Mmm, sure,' she said, feeling very relaxed from a full stomach and the excellent wine.

They sipped at the fiery liquid in silence, only the steady thrum of the waves intruding into the quietness. She realised how much she had missed this aspect of their friendship. The intimate conversations. Even the comfortable silences.

She stared at him over the rim of her glass, aware suddenly of his intense blue stare. The queerest sensation started burning between her hipbones and she felt a pressure flare to life. A very familiar pressure.

Her eyes fell on the chessboard that sat on a low table in front of the bank of floor-to-ceiling windows that separated the deck from the house. She'd never felt so much like kissing an inanimate object. They needed to keep occupied. Something was happening that shouldn't be.

'How about a game?' She indicated the board with a nod of her head.

Game? Sure. He could think of plenty. Strip chess sounded good, he thought as the butterfly swung tantalisingly against the swell of her breasts. When had the night gone from companionable to combustible? 'Sure,' he said, clearing his throat.

They moved to the other table and sat opposite each other.

'White or black?' she asked, admiring the familiar, intricate wooden pieces.

'Your choice,' he said.

'We'll draw for it,' she said picking up a white and a black piece and shifting them between her hands behind her back.

The action thrust her chest slightly forward and emphasised the glorious outline of her breasts. The butterfly got caught in her cleavage temporarily and Daniel suppressed the urge to lean forward and release it from its fleshy prison.

She thrust her downturned fists towards him. 'You pick,' she invited.

He tapped her right hand and she turned it over to reveal a white rook. 'You go first.' She smiled.

He was grateful to get the game under way, desperately needing a distraction. Not that it seemed to work. The damn butterfly messed up his concentration and it was no wonder she checkmated him quite early in the game.

'Rematch?' he asked.

What the hell? thought Sophie. Why not? It was great to play chess with someone who wasn't such a stickler for strategy. She and John still played quite a bit but he was very rigid and didn't like a lot of chat while playing, preferring to concentrate. At least with Daniel they could play and talk at the same time.

The second game was over quickly. Daniel shut down all thoughts other than victory and had her beaten in ten minutes.

'Checkmate,' he said triumphantly.

She eyed the board sceptically from every angle. She hadn't even seen that one coming. How had he done that? Her concentration was broken by Daniel's laughter.

'You haven't changed one bit.' He chuckled. 'Still as competitive as ever. Still disbelieving that anyone could beat you. Just like when we were kids.'

'Watch it or I'll tip the board up,' she threatened lightly. 'John's not here to pick on me for being a bad sport.'

They laughed together and Sophie couldn't help but be flooded by memories. They'd had such great times once. She sobered a little at how different things were now. How simple everything had been when they'd been younger.

She felt absurdly like crying and felt tears well in her eyes. She blinked them away but to her dismay one fell down her cheek unchecked. She turned away from Daniel, getting out of the chair and moving the short space to the bank of windows that led to the deck. The moonlit ocean shimmered through her tears.

Daniel rose, cursing himself as he went to comfort her. Her tears were surprising but, then, she'd had an emotional day. And he'd gone and brought up their childhood—memories that must still cause her heartache.

'Sophie,' he said quietly, coming up behind her and touching her shoulder.

She turned to face him. 'I'm sorry, Daniel. Don't worry about me, I'm fine. I don't know what's the matter with me lately.'

She looked so confused and they were so close. Close enough for him to wipe away the next tear that spilled from her lashes. Even though he knew he shouldn't.

Sophie felt strangely energised as his thumb moved across her cheek, gently capturing the tear. Something was happening. She held her breath as his fingers reached out and gently lifted the silver butterfly off her suddenly burning skin. He fingered it gently for a few moments and then placed it back onto the swell of her breast.

She sucked in a breath as his fingers lingered there, stroking the feverish skin lightly. Hot desire lanced her like a thrust from a dagger. She felt a tingling deep inside her and knew with sudden clarity that she needed him inside her like she needed her next breath.

Daniel's eyes widened at the pure sexual need reflected in her eyes. He *really* shouldn't be doing this. He needed to stop. Now! Somewhere inside him there was still a skerrick of sense telling him to step back.

But her skin felt so soft beneath his fingers and her perfume was mixing with another powerful essence—that of a woman ready for pleasure. His nostrils flared as they filled with the intoxicating scent. Even so, he knew he still possessed enough control to walk away.

'Danny,' she half groaned, half whispered, her voice

husky, her lips moist and swollen as her teeth bit into her bottom lip.

Now he was lost. No one but his grandfather called him Danny. But the way she said it, full of need and aching and promise, totally undid him.

He swooped his head down and claimed her mouth, closing the distance between them in an instant. Crushing her sweet skin against his. Desire exploded inside him as she opened her mouth to the urgent demand of his tongue. Fireworks sizzled and sparkled behind his eyes as his need to feel every inch of her against him had him pushing her hard against the glass. Closer. He had to get closer.

Sophie understood his need to get closer as she yanked his shirt out of his trousers and tore at the buttons until she could feel the glide of his smooth naked flesh under her hands.

'Oh, Danny. Danny!' she groaned, as the feel of his chest stirred her primal lust. She wanted him, needed him, and only the feel of him hard and hot and thrusting was going to obliterate it. 'I need you, Danny. Now!' she gasped, and fumbled with his belt buckle.

His kisses were driving her mad. His hand up her shirt, yanking her bra aside and rubbing her impossibly erect nipple, had her screaming for more. 'Help me,' she cried in frustration as desire rendered her fingers useless.

'Slow down,' he gasped, and laughed huskily as he helped her with his belt and zipper.

'No, Danny. If you don't come in me right now, I'm going to die.' And she kissed him again. Hot and long and deep, thrusting her hands into his underpants and grabbing his erection triumphantly. 'Danny,' she whimpered softly.

For heaven's sake, they were both standing half-naked

up against a glass wall like sex-crazed teenagers. 'Sophie…slow down,' he panted into her neck covering her hands where they were stroking him.

She shoved him half away from her. 'I'm serious, Danny. I need you like I need oxygen.'

'I want you, too,' he gasped, his chest heaving.

'Please, Danny, now,' she breathed, and pushed aside his clothing until he was blissfully free of any restrictions and completely hers to touch.

Sophie couldn't explain it. She didn't understand it. All she knew was that if she didn't feel the hardness she held in her hand inside her in the next second she would scream. She didn't care whether she orgasmed or not. This was beyond the need for gratification. This was something primal. And it was such a turn-on she could hardly see straight.

'Danny!' she demanded again.

He didn't usually operate this way. He always gave pleasure before he took it. Always. But the caveman in him was emerging with Sophie's desperate urgings and he felt his desire surge to new heights. There was something passionate about a woman wanting you inside her this badly.

He pushed her pants aside impatiently and groaned into her mouth as he plunged his fingers into her heat.

She practically screamed into his mouth and he felt her legs buckle. He quickly shoved her further up the wall.

'No. Please, Danny. This. I want this,' she breathed, pushing him to her entrance, squirming and grinding her hips against his swollen erection.

He entered her in one swift movement, no longer able to deny his body or hers the thing they both wanted. He heard her cry out and almost roared in triumph as her tightness captured him and stroked him. He kissed her harshly, brutally almost, as her wild urgings and moans hurtled him close to his release.

There was something incredibly primitive and ardent about their act. Her head bumped against the glass as each thrust drove her against it. The silver butterfly moved in unison as he yanked her shirt aside and feasted on an engorged nipple.

Sophie was a whimpering mass of nerve endings. Her eyes rolled back as the pressure inside her was caressed by each masterstroke from Daniel. His wet mouth taunting her nipple was almost too much to bear and Sophie knew she was going to faint from the sheer sating of her need.

She cried out as the unbearable pressure ruptured and released inside her. The pleasure wave surged through her with all the power and force of a tornado. She heard and felt him as he joined her and together they rode the almighty heights as it took them to the stars and back.

It took an age to float back down to earth. Their ragged breathing was the only noise in the room. Daniel had slumped against Sophie, his chest heaving, his head burrowed into her shoulder as her sated body relaxed against him and he supported her weight.

They were still joined. He could still feel her internal muscles as they sporadically pulsed around him. It felt incredibly erotic and made it impossible for his erection to settle. Never in his wildest dreams had he imagined it could be this good.

Their breathing took for ever to settle. Sophie could feel Daniel still hard inside her, the length of him teasing her already sensitive nerve endings. She could feel her arousal build again, her release of a few moments ago already not enough. It had been two long years and she didn't want to let go of this moment. Not yet.

She moved against him and felt his instantaneous response.

'Sophie,' he moaned into her shoulder.

She kissed his head, her face caressed by the soft, fine hair, and moved again.

'Sophie.' His voice held a desperate strangled note and he raised his head to look at her.

'More,' she said huskily.

'More?'

'More,' she said, and moved again as she lowered her head and gave him a deep lingering kiss.

'Not like this,' he said, releasing her and lowering her to the floor.

'Please, Danny,' she whispered. She needed him again.

'My way this time,' he whispered back, kissing her swollen mouth and swinging her up into his arms.

He placed her gently on his bed, kissing her deeply before pulling away and stripping off his clothes. He helped her off with hers and it was the most amazing feeling to be totally naked with her again. Just like old times. She was looking at him like she always had—with pure desire. And he felt the thrumming of his blood pound in anticipation.

He took his time, rediscovering every inch of her body. All the places that made her shiver, the ones that made her skin goosy and the ones that made her cry out loud. Her neck, her knees, her breasts and finally her moist centre.

When her orgasm arched her back and tore through her body it was his mouth that swallowed her cries and his mouth that kissed her eyes as tears fell on her cheeks and his mouth that covered hers with tiny butterfly kisses until the last whimper had left her lips.

And then, just as she was getting her head around the mind-blowing pleasure he had unleashed upon her, she felt his erection nudging her as he pushed himself into her. She took him to the hilt, kissing him, and a surge of moisture inside her caused him to groan into her mouth.

'Sophie,' he muttered, breaking away from her kiss.

'Oh, yes, Danny,' she whispered, opening her eyes to find him staring at her, his blue eyes glazed with passion.

'Sophie,' he muttered again, incredibly turned on by her flushed cheeks and the swollen moistness of her bottom lip and the look of complete abandonment.

'Don't stop,' she begged, hypnotised by the passion in his stare.

His breathing became rough and unsteady again with each stroke into her tightness.

'Oh, Danny. Yes. I'm—I'm…'

'Me, too,' he breathed, feeling his body start to tremble uncontrollably as he claimed her mouth and with one final thrust brought the sky shattering down around them.

Sophie felt like she'd left her body as the pleasure undulated through her. Sharp and intense at first and then deep and slow as the first manic surge ebbed. She could hear their mingled cries somewhere below her but her thundering heartbeat obliterated all other noises.

And somewhere between flying up into the stratosphere and floating back to the ground, Sophie realised the horrible truth. She still loved him. Nothing had changed. It was just like old times.

Making love to him was one thing but *falling* in love? That was going to be a lot harder to rationalise.

CHAPTER EIGHT

THEIR breathing settled more quickly this time and Sophie felt a malaise invade her bones. Daniel took a couple of deep breaths and slowly pushed himself away from her. They stared at each other wordlessly, their breathing almost normal.

'What happens now?' Daniel asked.

Sophie shrugged and licked her lips and noticed the flare in Daniel's eyes as he followed the motion. What had they done? How were they ever going to be brother and sister-in-law again?

'I don't know, Daniel,' she said, sitting up and dragging the sheet around her. 'I don't have a guide book about what to do after you've just had sex with your dead husband's brother.'

She hadn't meant it to sound so callous but she couldn't remember ever feeling this confused. Not even after he had so suddenly rejected her all those years ago. How could they have done this again and how could she have been in love with him all these years and not realised it? But she knew without a doubt that she'd never stopped loving him.

He flinched at the harshness of her words. Wasn't he more than that? He watched as she avoided looking at him—she regretted it already. He nodded slowly. 'We shouldn't have done it,' he said matter-of-factly, massaging his temples.

She closed her eyes as his words wounded—he regretted it already. Oh, God! She couldn't bear a repeat of the recriminations that had happened when they had succumbed to temptation hours after Michael's funeral.

Sophie felt herself becoming angry. She wanted to yell, Of course we shouldn't have done it, but I love you, you idiot, and it's not how I loved your brother. It's all-consuming, it's in every cell of my body and every fibre of my being. It even hurts to breathe when I think about it.

'Of course we shouldn't have,' she said into the silence because she'd be damned if he'd hurt her with his words again. She was getting in first this time. 'Maybe if you hadn't taken advantage of my vulnerability, it wouldn't have happened at all.'

'I'm sorry?' Daniel's fingers stilled. What exactly did she mean by that?

'I was upset about Beryl…you knew that.'

'No. Wait. I didn't do anything that you didn't want me to do. Begged me to do.' His blue eyes glittered dangerously.

She had made him angry. Good! Maybe he could taste some of how she was feeling.

'I was grieving, Daniel. No one thinks straight in that frame of mind.'

'Grieving? That's a bit strong, isn't it? Upset, maybe. She was just a patient, Sophie. It wasn't—'

'Who? Michael? Hmm, yes, I'm seeing a pattern here.

You pop up in my life at significant sad moments, have sex with me and then tell me you shouldn't have done it.'

'Sophie, it's not like that.'

'Really? Oh, no, that's right. It's usually my fault. How could I do it to you—et cetera, et cetera? That's right. I'm remembering now.'

'I think you're being a little unfair. I've told you I was sorry for what I said to you after Michael's funeral. And I don't feel that what just happened now is the same thing. But, Sophie, we can't keep doing this. It's not right.'

'Doing what, Daniel? What are we doing?'

'Playing with fire. That's what. You are my brother's wife—'

'No. I am your brother's widow.'

'It doesn't matter. There can never be anything between us, Sophie. There's too much history and too much angst. And it's just too…complicated!'

They stared at each other for a few more moments. Sophie felt her body stirring again. She almost screamed out loud at the unfairness of it all. Here she was in bed with the person she loved and a dead man stood between them.

'And what if I still love you, Daniel? What happens then?' It was impossible. She couldn't love him. She shouldn't. Tears tracked down her face. And, funnily enough, she didn't care. This situation was crazy and if they didn't get some resolution, they'd need to send for the men in white coats.

'Don't be ridiculous, Sophie. You don't love me. You love Michael.' He needed to hang onto that. That was how it was supposed to be. It was the only thing that had kept him away for four years. 'We both love him and we can't do this to him. He deserves our loyalty not our disrespect. What we just did, twice, is disrespectful to his memory.'

Daniel held onto his belief. He'd stuffed up his brother's life and the guilt had never gone away. He owed him and he'd struggled with that obligation ever since. He'd even given up Sophie for Michael. And now he was dead, a death that wouldn't have happened had he not been confined to that damned wheelchair. The wheelchair that *he* had put him in.

Had his death changed things? No. If anything, Daniel felt it demanded a greater commitment from him. Just because his brother was gone, it didn't negate *his* obligation, and he was damned if he was going to let Michael down again.

Sophie was talking crazily. It was easy to confuse feelings from the past when the intimacies they had shared were still so fresh. But his feelings were exactly that—in the past.

'Don't tell me what I feel.'

'You'll feel differently tomorrow. You just need a bit of perspective.'

Was he mad? Did he really believe that? Sophie looked at him with fresh eyes. He did. She could see the almost zealous belief stamped on his face and she knew that nothing she could say to him tonight would make a blind bit of difference.

Well, that was fine, but she loved him and she didn't want to sit around and have him talk her out of it. She had to get out of here. Daniel had broken her heart one too many times and she wasn't about to start hitting her head against the wall, waiting for him to throw her some crumbs.

He had told her four years ago that he didn't love her,

and despite her utter devastation she had survived. And she would do it again.

She slid out of bed and walked out of the room. He let her go, quelling the urge to call her back. He wasn't sure what had just happened but it was obvious she was upset. If he could start the night over he would, but what was done was done.

He loaded the dishes into the dishwasher and tidied the kitchen. His first instinct was to flee back to New York. But he'd promised John he would stay for as long as his recovery took and then there was the pledge he had made himself about being around for Max. Going back wasn't an option.

'I'm going.'

Sophie's voice pulled him out of his thoughts and he focussed on her, noting her packed bag at her feet. 'No, Soph. Please, don't leave.'

'I can't stay,' she said huskily, picking up the bag and walking away before she changed her mind and threw herself at his feet and begged him to love her.

Daniel stayed still, listening to the door shut and then, a few moments later, her car drive away. Damn! He'd handled that really badly. They'd been close tonight, before they'd ruined it by becoming physical. And while the intimacy had been fantastic, the feeling that they had been on the road to rebuilding their friendship had been better.

He didn't want it to end like this. He threw down the teatowel he was holding, quickly switched out the lights and locked the door behind him. He didn't have time to shut up properly and would have to remember to talk to Charlie about it in the morning. Right now all he cared about was catching up with Sophie and making her see sense.

He estimated he was maybe fifteen minutes behind her as he got into his car. It was nine p.m. so traffic wasn't going to be a problem. He was glad when he reached the gate to the property and turned out onto the main road. He'd have a chance to really accelerate now.

He caught up with her yellow VW on the highway back to Brisbane and reduced his speed to sit behind her until the highway exit. There was really no where for them to pull over on the dual carriageway so he'd have to cool his heels for the next hour or so.

He didn't want them to go back to their corners and prepare for the next round. He was tired of the continual undercurrent of blame and anger. Whether it had been wise or not, they had crossed a line tonight that neither of them could ignore. They had to find a way to accept their mistake and go on with their lives.

Because they were involved with each other, whether they liked it or not. They were family, and while it had been much easier when a whole world had separated them, that was no longer the case. He was going to be around a lot, for John and for Max, and they had to finally deal with it. Tonight.

Sophie didn't realise it was Daniel's car behind her and even if she had been aware of it her tears wouldn't have allowed her a clear view. How many types of fool were there in the world? How many times was she bound to make the same mistake? When would she learn that falling in love with Daniel Monday was always doomed to fail?

Apart from a few brief happy months when they had been lovers and a son he didn't realise he had, Daniel had caused her no end of heartache these last four years. She had thought her defences against him were rock solid and had been prepared for any new onslaught he could possibly unleash. But solid defences didn't help you if the enemy lurked within!

Fresh tears fell as she berated herself for her foolishness. When she had told Daniel she was one hundred per cent over him she had genuinely meant it. How could she have lied to herself all these years? He had never truly left her heart, she'd just managed to move into a state of extreme denial. Damn it, she swore silently, and slammed one palm into the steering-wheel for good measure.

An ambulance flashed past her with its lights and sirens blazing, and it brought her out of her thoughts as she immediately eased her foot off the accelerator. She wondered where they were going and to what, and sent a little prayer heavenwards that no one was seriously ill or injured.

It became apparent a few minutes later as she rounded a bend that her prayer had been too late. She braked gently as a scene of total road carnage greeted her. Three cars, one turned over, the others smashed and twisted, lay scattered on the highway. Broken glass, car parts and walking wounded added to the scene of devastation. A lone policeman was controlling traffic and the ambulance that had passed her was the only one on the scene.

Sophie pulled to the side of the road, thinking she could help a little before reinforcements arrived. She got out of her car and was making her way towards the scene when a familiar voice called her name.

'Sophie.'

She turned and saw Daniel walking towards her. 'Daniel?' Despite the situation, she felt her stomach flip-flop. How had he got here? But now wasn't the time for questions or to pick up where they had left off, and they both knew it. People needed them and that took priority.

The policeman tried to stop them as they walked quickly into the fray. 'Step back, please,' he ordered. 'Go back to your vehicles.'

'I'm a paramedic and Sophie's an emergency nurse. We just thought the crew over there could do with a hand,' said Daniel.

The young policeman hesitated for a second.

'Come on, mate, they're snowed under. At least let us help until some back-up arrives.'

The policeman waved them through and they raced over to one of the paramedics. It was Jane Carter, the ICP who had helped that night in the rain with Charlie.

'Am I glad to see you guys,' she said, recognising them instantly and giving them each a pop-over vest with AMBULANCE emblazoned in reflective lettering front and back. 'There's twelve victims from three cars as far as we've been able to assess. We're trying to triage at the moment. There's two entrapments, one in a bad way, the other negative. The rest appear to be relatively unscathed. If you guys could do some quick head to toes on them, that will free me and my partner up to deal with the girl who's trapped in her vehicle.'

'How far away is your back-up?' asked Sophie.

'Another fifteen minutes,' Jane replied, before heading off to the flattened car where a human being's life hung in the balance.

Daniel and Sophie worked as a team, organising those who could walk to sit by the ambulance where the light was best and they could assess them more easily. They put cervical collars on as many people as they could, checked neurological states and looked for broken bones and haemorrhages.

Several fire engines arrived, adding to the colourful strobing of lights. Sophie heard the guttural growl of a motor starting up in the background, followed by the crunching of metal as the jaws of life sliced through the frame of a vehicle as if it were a tin can. It wouldn't be long now until the girl was released from her squashed car.

Three ambulances pulled up, shining their headlights across the carnage and into the night, the glass on the road sparkling like diamonds in the glare. Several paramedics descended upon them and Daniel gratefully handed their patients over.

As the ambulances began to leave with the injured Sophie noticed a girl she hadn't seen before wandering around aimlessly. She had some dried blood on her forehead and was muttering to herself. She had panda-like eyes where tears had mingled with her mascara, causing it to run.

'Hi, I'm Sophie. Were you involved in the accident? How about you come over to the ambulance and we can check you out?'

The girl, who looked about nineteen, stared at her blankly. She seemed dazed and Sophie was concerned that she might be concussed.

'James. I can't find James,' she said, looking straight through Sophie.

Sophie felt a prickle of alarm. 'Was James in the car with you?' she asked gently.

'He was driving,' she said absently.

Sophie searched her memory. The name didn't ring a bell from any of the people she had treated tonight, but she hadn't seen them all. Maybe Daniel had treated him?

She led the confused young woman over to Daniel, reaching into the back of the ambulance to grab a blanket and put it around her patient's slim shoulders. The girl was shaking and was obviously shocked.

'Daniel, did you treat anyone called James tonight?'

'No,' said Daniel, automatically checking out the girl, concern creasing his brow. 'What's your name?' he asked as he shone a penlight into her eyes, relieved to find her pupils equal and reactive.

'Donna,' she said. 'I'm fine, really, I had my seat belt on but James didn't. I told him he should put it on…I told him.'

Daniel flicked a glance at Sophie and she knew, without asking him, what he wanted. She located the scene controller and informed him they'd have to search the area for another potential patient.

Sophie and Daniel joined in the search along with available fire crews and police. Torches in hand, they searched the overgrown nature strips either side of the highway, the beams of light probing the darkness.

'Found him,' a voice called, and Sophie and Daniel rushed to the ditch, where James had been thrown clear of his car.

Daniel took one look at the young man and knew he was dead. His body was twisted at an awkward angle and his head skewed in the opposite direction. A sudden vision of Michael's body lying on the road flashed into his mind, and Daniel blinked hard to erase it.

Donna had managed to break through the crowd surrounding James's body. She threw herself on the ground and knelt over the inert form. He appeared to be about the same age as her.

'James, James!' she yelled frantically, shaking his body. 'Help him. Help him,' she begged, looking at Daniel with wild, frightened eyes. 'Why won't he wake up? He won't wake up.' She intermittently shook his body and wrung her hands.

A few of the searchers tried to pull her back but Daniel signalled to them to leave her. The girl grabbed Daniel's hand and yanked him down beside her.

'Fix him,' she begged, pushing his hands onto the young man's chest.

Sophie sank to her knees beside Donna and put her arm around the girl's shoulders.

Daniel looked at Sophie wordlessly and she shrugged, knowing that the situation was futile but also knowing that Donna needed to see something being done.

Daniel placed his fingers over the young man's carotid pulse. Absent. He put his stethoscope in his ears and placed it on the dead man's chest. Breathing—absent. Heartbeat—absent. He'd broken his neck and had probably died instantly.

Starting any resuscitation measures now would be futile and probably not welcomed by this fit-looking young man who would, if by some miracle they were successful, spend the rest of his life in a wheelchair hooked up to a ventilator with major brain damage.

He thought about how angry Michael had been that Daniel had resuscitated him at the scene of their accident, only to be left a paraplegic.

'James,' Donna sniffed, wiping her eyes, smearing her

mascara further. 'You can help him, can't you?' she pleaded, choking on her sobs as Daniel removed the stethoscope from his ears.

'James is dead. I'm very sorry. He's broken his neck.' Daniel's voice was gentle as he covered her hand that gripped his arm. It was a horrible thing to have to tell her in less than ideal surroundings.

'No, no.' She shook her head violently from side to side, looking from Daniel to Sophie and back to Daniel again. 'No. You have to fix him. You have to make him wake up. I didn't get to tell him I loved him. You have to make him wake up!' She was sobbing hysterically now, and shaking Daniel's arm.

'I'm sorry, there's nothing I can do,' he said quietly.

Her face crumpled and she let out a cry of such agony that it raised goose-bumps on Daniel's arms. She threw herself at her boyfriend's body, her head against his chest, her hands clutching his shoulders.

'No, James. No,' she sobbed. 'I love you. I love you. Can you hear me? Don't leave me. I love you.'

Daniel and Sophie sat with the girl as she wept, and the small crowd of people surrounding them peeled away, knowing there was nothing further they could do. The scene controller, in his fluorescent yellow vest, approached.

'Your patient?' he asked Daniel.

'Negative,' Daniel said softly, and the man nodded and backed away.

An over-zealous official brought a sheet to place over the body, but Daniel waved him away. Donna was still holding onto James. The girl needed time to grieve, she would let him go when she was ready.

The girl's cries were chilling. She kept touching her boyfriend's face as if the sheer depth of her love alone could bring him back. She kept asking, 'Why? Why didn't I tell you?'

Sophie blinked back tears as the young woman's grief chilled her to the core. She looked away, the intensity of Donna's grief almost too painful to witness.

She surveyed the carnage of the three-car pile-up strewn all over the highway. Twisted car bodies, stray pieces of luggage, personal items and broken glass littered the road surface. A multitude of flashing lights strobed into the night like glitter balls at a gruesome discotheque.

Two young people lay dead from a lethal mix of alcohol and no seat belts. Ten others had been very lucky to escape major injury. What a waste of life.

They stayed with the girl until she had cried herself out, neither of them wanting to leave her in such an overwrought state. She eventually let go of James's body and allowed Sophie to take her to a waiting ambulance.

Sophie caught a glimpse of the utterly defeated young woman before the back doors slammed and they took her to St Jude's for observation. She looked small and forlorn, her panda eyes all but gone now—a million tears having washed the mascara away altogether.

Sophie knew what Donna was going through. Knew how the suddenness of death sucked your breath away, how your mind reeled and you couldn't take in the awful truth. How, just when you thought you'd finished crying and there could not possibly be any more tears left, they came again. And again.

Sophie leant against her car now there was nothing for

her to do, and waited for Daniel to finish talking to the accident investigation squad. She had already given her statement. The road was obviously going to be blocked for hours as nothing could be moved until the investigation was complete.

After what had happened at the beach house she should just get in her car and go. Take the detour the police had set up and drive home to Arabella. But she couldn't. As mad as she was at Daniel, at the moment part of her knew that James's death had to have been hard for him.

Sure, he'd been the consummate professional tonight but something like that was just too close to home. There must have been some memories stirred for him.

'You OK?' he asked half an hour later as he approached her. He remembered her quietness after the Sunvalley house fire and how she had been affected by the rawness of his job. Well, this had been pretty raw, too.

'Sure,' she said. 'What about you?'

'What about me?' He smiled.

'I thought the whole James thing might be a little confronting for you.'

'Ah,' he said. She was astute. She was leaning against her car for support and he copied her pose, standing beside her, their arms brushing lightly.

They didn't speak for a while. The incident at the beach house had taken a back seat. Their minds were full of the carnage they had witnessed and the people they had treated and the two young people who weren't going home tonight, or any night.

And another car accident four years ago that had dramatically altered the course of their lives for ever.

'I could have tried to resuscitate him,' said Daniel into the now eerily quiet night air.

'It was too late, Daniel. He'd broken his neck. Too much time had elapsed. You know you wouldn't have got him back.'

'I resuscitated Michael.'

'It's different, and you know it. You were right there, you were able to administer immediate first aid to Michael. James had been in that ditch for who knows how long. Besides, Michael's spinal cord injury was much lower. We didn't need a CAT scan or an MRI to tell us that. People's heads don't twist that far unless something's snapped.'

Daniel nodded. 'I just kept seeing Michael's face,' he whispered. 'Remembering that night.'

'It wasn't your fault, Daniel.'

'Of course it was. I was driving.'

'A man had a heart attack at the wheel on the opposite side of the road, veered across into your lane and smashed into you. It was a freak accident.'

'Well, why do I still feel so guilty?'

'I don't know, Daniel. Why do you?'

He was silent for a moment. 'Because I was thinking about you, that's why, when the other car veered. And I know it all happened very suddenly but maybe if I hadn't been so preoccupied with you and how great you looked naked and how wonderful you smelt and how lucky I was to have you, then maybe I would have seen it coming sooner. Maybe I could have swerved or braked or done anything other than let it happen.'

Sophie swallowed the lump in her throat. She heard the anguish and accusation in his voice. So it had been her fault? No. She wasn't going to take that on. She couldn't

control who was thinking about her and when, and if
Daniel really thought a split second would have made a difference to the outcome of their accident, he was crazy.

'I was looking into James's face tonight and Donna was
begging me to do something, and all I could hear was
Michael yelling at me how I should have let him die, and
I just couldn't put James through that.'

Sophie remembered the anger and the bitterness that
Michael had felt in that first month and how in the deepest part of his depression he had said those things to Daniel
and had even begged her to help him end his life.

She looked at the man she loved and felt his pain. 'You
did what anyone would have done, especially a paramedic.
Especially a brother. Michael went on to have a full and
happy and productive life. James would be a ventilator-de-
pendent quadriplegic.'

'I know…I know,' he sighed, and turned on his side so
he was facing her. 'It just kind of sucks, though, doesn't it?'

'Absolutely,' she agreed, turning to face him also. 'It
does. But it doesn't make it your fault. What happened with
Michael was just coincidence. Two sets of strangers in the
wrong place at the wrong time. There's no rhyme or reason
to it. It was bad luck. That's all. And, yes, that sucks, too.'

She rose on tiptoe to kiss him on the cheek. It was a platonic gesture because she couldn't bear it that he still
blamed himself for something that had been a tragic accident, and wanted to comfort him somehow.

But she knew even before she reached his face that it
would be his mouth she would kiss. Something compelled
her and with the memory of their love-making so fresh it
was an urge she couldn't quell. She pressed her lips against

his and then pulled back slightly. She felt reaction to the kiss slam into her and saw his nostrils flare and his eyes glaze.

She kissed him again and felt her lips open to the demanding pressure of his. His arm came around her waist, drawing her against him, and Sophie felt her head bend further back as the heat from his mouth drugged her into submission. Her heartbeat pounded in her ears and she could feel her internal muscles stir to life again. Man! Could he kiss!

With a supreme effort she broke away and they shared an unfathomable look, chests heaving.

'I'm going home now,' she said huskily. She opened the door and got in, and Daniel crouched beside her window. She pressed the button and the glass whirred down.

'Drive carefully, Soph,' he said quietly, his blue-eyed stare mesmerising. It wasn't something he needed to say with the horror of the night still close. 'And kiss Max for me.'

She drove off, his last words reminding her of yet another reason why she loved him. Their son. Their beautiful Max.

She sure didn't make things easy for herself. She was in love with someone she shouldn't be in love with. Someone whose emotional commitment to his brother was steeped in guilt so thick that it prevented him from feeling and loving freely.

Sophie despaired at what she could do to change it. She had a feeling that only Michael himself could release Daniel from his self-imposed feelings of obligation. And Michael was dead. It didn't bode well.

pliment. It was also true. Taking blood and putting in IVs were skills she had mastered.

Mrs Schmidt lay docilely on the trolley, staring into space.

'How was she when you tried?' she asked Karen.

'Quiet as a lamb.'

Still, Sophie gloved up with some trepidation. The woman lying on the trolley was a far cry from the agitated patient who had come into the department a couple of months ago, but she didn't really want a repeat performance.

'She seems a lot calmer,' commented Sophie to Anna.

'Oh, yes. She's much easier to handle now. The geriatric team said there wasn't a whole lot they could do for her as her dementia was quite advanced, but they put her on some medication and it's really helped. Coming here that night was a godsend, Sister. I was at the end of my tether.'

'That's excellent.' Sophie smiled. 'What brings you here today?'

'Well, I was a bit worried that she's over-medicated. She's been very sleepy the last few days and is often hard to rouse. I rang the geriatric doctor and he advised me to come here and have some drug levels done.'

Sophie nodded and snapped on the tourniquet. Karen held Mrs Schmidt's arm and Anna stood on the other side, ready if the old lady let fly again.

Sophie prodded the crook of her patient's arm with her gloved fingers. Taking blood, particularly from difficult veins, with gloves on made the job even harder. The latex barrier really reduced the ability to 'feel' a vein.

Concentration creased Sophie's brow as she thought she felt one quite deep. There were several closer to the skin surface but Sophie could feel the knotting and guessed they were probably too sclerosed to be of any use.

She took a breath and slid the needle in. Mrs Schmidt didn't even flinch and Sophie closed her eyes as she advanced the needle deeper, sensing the vein position as much as feeling it. She got a flashback and almost whooped as dark red blood filled the syringe.

Mrs Schmidt remained docile throughout the procedure and Sophie felt admiration for Anna. After the months of abuse she'd had from her grandmother she could be forgiven for wanting docility. But she obviously loved the old lady a lot and preferred to see a happy balance rather than an extreme either way.

Sophie shut the curtains behind her and placed the blood tubes and path form in the box that was regularly collected by a pathology courier. She spied Daniel coming in through the ambulance bay and her stomach flopped at the sight of his long-legged stride, reminding her of her one and only ride on a roller-coaster.

Memories from the other night came flooding back, making it impossible to get off the ride. How he had felt inside her, how good his lips had felt on her breast, how erotic it felt to be pinned high against the glass by the force of his surging desire.

He chose that moment to look up and fix her with a blue stare. She knew his thoughts were on that night, too. The look of pure sexual hunger transmitted in his stare had her stomach looping the loop. She felt her cheeks grow warm as his lustful gaze continued.

'Sophie.' He nodded, still staring as he drew the trolley to a halt beside her.

'Daniel.' She tried to steady her voice but even to her own ears she sounded like a swooning heroine from an old black-and-white movie.

They stared at each other for a few more moments until Ben, the other paramedic, cleared his throat loudly. Daniel gave himself a mental shake. 'Unknown female. Probably early twenties. Found OD'd in the valley. Probably heroin. Not a known junkie. No track marks. Given Narcan after some bag-masking failed to produce a response. She is rousable. Haven't been able to identify her or elicit any info from her. I inserted an IV at the scene.'

Sophie watched his lips move as he formed his words. She tried not to stare at them or think about the magic they had weaved.

'Sophie?' he prompted quietly.

'Hmm? Oh, yes…right,' she said, dragging her eyes away to look at the patient on the trolley. The woman was lying on her side and had on an oxygen mask. An oropharyngeal airway protruded from between her lips. A white cellular blanket covered her slight form.

'Oh, my God. It's Jenny.' Sophie recognised her instantly as they pushed the trolley into a cubicle. 'She was a patient here a few months ago. She'd been raped by two men. Jenny? Jenny, can you hear me?' Sophie spoke loudly as she shook the girl's shoulder firmly. 'Jenny. Open your eyes and talk to me.'

The patient roused at the insistent note in Sophie's voice and coughed on the airway, which she promptly spat out as she pulled the mask away. She tried to sit up, obviously disorientated from the side effects of the drug.

She was as tiny as Sophie remembered. Maybe more so,

her arms looking almost skeletal. But she was a far cry from the woman who had presented to the department a few months ago. That Jenny's face had been swollen and bloodied, her upper lip cut and a nasty bruise had blackened her right eye. Her blouse had been torn and there had been grazing to her hands and arms.

'Where am I?' she asked.

'You're at St Jude's. It's Sophie. I looked after you when you came in before. Do you remember?'

'Oh, no, no, no,' Jenny groaned, and threw herself back as tears rolled down her cheeks. 'I don't want to be here. I just want to die. Just leave me to die.' Sobs choked from her throat as she curled herself into a ball.

Daniel lingered and watched Sophie for a few minutes as she worked. She leaned forward and spoke softly to her distraught patient. She held Jenny's hand and stroked it and was quick with the vomit bowl as Jenny started to retch.

She was professional and efficient and in control. Very different from the woman he had held the other night. Her blind need had brought her to a state of begging and he hardened, just thinking about how she had pleaded with him. Time to go!

A couple of hours later, after Jenny had had a chance to sleep and recoup, Sophie was able to talk to her. She brought her some juice to drink and some sandwiches.

'What happened today, Jenny?'

'I just couldn't stand it any longer.' A tear trickled down her cheek. 'I've just felt so dirty, so violated. The police haven't caught them yet and I see their faces in every man who passes. I'm so scared all the time.'

'What did you take?'

'I went to the valley because I'd heard you could get heroin there. I didn't want to just take a whole bunch of pills. I wanted to do it properly. I bought some off a dealer and he showed me how to inject it. I went back to the alley where…where…' She stopped and struggled to pull herself together.

'It just seemed fitting, you know? To die there. In that alley where they raped me. It seemed like the perfect place to end it all. I can't believe someone found me.'

Sophie put her arm around Jenny as she sobbed anew, and stayed until she had calmed down.

'Have you been going to your counselling sessions?'

Jenny shook her head. 'I can't talk about it with a complete stranger. How could they possibly know how I feel?'

'Remember how I told you the rape crisis counsellors are all women who have been raped? They have professional counselling qualifications and they specialise in rape recovery.'

'Really? I don't remember that,' said Jenny. Her voice wobbled as she dried her tears.

That was hardly surprising. It was hard to take everything in after such a vile act had been perpetrated against you. 'Really. And you know what? Sometimes it's easier to talk to someone you don't know than those close to you. Particularly if they've been through the same thing as you.'

Sophie rang the crisis centre at Jenny's request. A counsellor arrived promptly and Sophie left them to it. She hoped desperately that Jenny had taken a big step towards recovery tonight.

Sometimes people had to hit rock bottom before they

could climb back up again. Lying in an alley with a needle sticking out of your arm had hopefully been Jenny's.

With Jenny's issues as resolved as she could make them this shift, Sophie's thoughts returned to Daniel. The heat that had flared between them had taken her by surprise. She had understood her reaction but interestingly it definitely hadn't been one-sided. Maybe he wasn't as indifferent to her as he tried to make out.

A little while later, Sophie stood at the triage desk, chatting with Richard and Ross, the after-hours nurse manager. He had his pencil out and was tapping it against his teeth. Todd was at the other end of the desk, inputting data on the computer. The waiting room had all but emptied and in thirty minutes their shift would be over.

What happened next occurred so quickly that Sophie didn't have time to register it or even scream. Suddenly she felt the sharp edge of something cold and metallic pressed to her throat. A filthy arm grabbed her around the chest and dragged her backwards. Her nostrils filled with the fetid stench of unwashed skin.

'Don't move!' A chilling snarl cut through the confusion in her mind. It had happened too swiftly to assimilate all the messages coming from her brain.

'Nobody move,' the man roared, swinging wildly from side to side, yanking Sophie with him. 'Everyone stay calm. I'll let her go as soon as I get morphine. But I swear I'll cut her up right here in front of you all if you screw with me. Morphine! Now!'

Sophie swallowed hard and tried not to panic. He was a junkie. She could feel his violent trembling and smell the cold sweat covering his bony body. He needed a fix.

Obviously badly to pull this stunt. Her heart rate soared and she felt the knife point press a little closer to her jugular vein.

'Listen, mate,' said Richard, standing slowly and putting his hands out. 'Don't do anything crazy.'

'That's right,' said Todd, clearing his throat. 'Just take it easy.'

'Morphine,' the man roared again.

'It's not as easy as all that. There are procedures for dangerous drugs. Counts,' Ross hedged.

Sophie couldn't believe what she was hearing. She and Ross had never seen eye to eye. He typified a management stereotype that she'd never had much time for, but even so she would have expected his support in this instance.

Surely he was joking! OK, it was Ross's job to manage and this incident would swamp him in paperwork, but surely he could see through the bureaucratic haze long enough to know that the man with the knife was serious.

'Just get the drugs, Ross,' she hissed.

'You'd better listen to her, mister,' the junkie advised. 'All of it, everything in the cupboard.'

Sophie watched as Richard handed the drug-cupboard keys to Ross. Richard's eyes communicated his worry to her. He looked down quickly and pointedly and then looked back at her.

Sophie was confused at first and then remembered the panic button that had been installed beneath the triage desk last year. She shook her head imperceptibly at Richard. She was fairly certain that the arrival of several security guards would only worsen the situation.

She shut her eyes and thought, Please, don't let me die tonight. Max needed her. She thought about never seeing him again and couldn't breathe. He'd be well looked after, she knew that, and she guessed that John would tell Daniel the truth and Max would finally be with his father. But it wouldn't be fair to deprive a little boy of his mother, too.

Her life flashed before her and she thought about all the other people she would miss. John and Michael's parents and Sally and Charlie. And Daniel. What if she never saw Daniel again? What if she never got the chance to tell him she loved him?

'Sophie!'

Daniel's voice. Had her fear and panic managed to conjure him up? Was he real? She opened her eyes and there he was.

'Stop right there, mate.' The guy sounded panicky at Daniel's arrival. 'I'll kill her. I swear it. Where's my drugs?' he roared in Sophie's ear, and she shut her eyes again.

Daniel stood beside the trolley he'd been bringing in, immobilised with fear. Sophie. His Sophie being pawed by a man with a dirty, rusty kitchen knife held to her throat. She looked frightened and pale and Daniel felt fear and then rage build inside him.

'What's taking him so long?' Sophie's attacker yelled.

Daniel spied an insipid-looking man standing at the end of the corridor, drugs in hand, talking to four security guards. For heaven's sake! Who had rung them?

Four years in New York had given Daniel lots of experience with drug addicts and how desperate they could be. Any signs of force could panic them and that made them unpredictable.

The man was obviously close to the edge. His eyes were darting around the room and there was sweat running down his pale, sickly face. Daniel felt ill. The fear on the beautiful face of the woman he loved twisted in his gut.

And there it was. A true light-bulb moment. The woman he loved. It was as if there had been an invisible curtain between them all this time and it had taken one drug-crazed lunatic to tear it down and reveal the truth. He loved her. It was so simple and so powerful all at the same time.

'Stay back,' Daniel commanded the security guards in a loud voice. 'He's got a knife and he'll use it.'

The junkie swung around nervously, sensing he was about to lose control of the situation. 'Listen to him,' he shouted. 'I'll cut her. I swear it!'

'You. Bring the drugs—now!' Daniel's demand brooked no argument.

Sophie held her breath and felt tears threaten. She would not cry. Tears weren't going to help now. She needed to think clearly. Thank God Daniel had arrived. He was taking charge of the situation and she began to feel like it might just turn out OK. If only Ross complied.

Daniel had had enough. If this guy walked any slower down the corridor he'd arrive some time tomorrow. He strode off and seized the drugs from him, shooting Ross a look of pure contempt. As far as human beings went, Daniel thought, he was a waste of good oxygen.

He turned around and in five large strides was back at the triage desk, holding the boxes of morphine out to Sophie's captor.

'Let her go,' he demanded, his heart banging loudly.

'Give me the drugs first. Put them in the bag,' he said, dropping a filthy backpack off his shoulder to the floor and kicking it towards Daniel.

Daniel stuffed the boxes inside.

'Kick it back.'

Daniel did as he was told and the junkie slowly reached down and gathered it up.

'Let her go,' Daniel demanded again.

The man smiled triumphantly and licked his lips, showing a bunch of yellowed rotting teeth. He pushed Sophie away with a force that belied his state of ill health and ran towards the door, but before he could even make good his escape the security guards had tackled him to the ground.

Sophie crashed into Daniel's body and he pulled her to him, crushing her against him as overwhelming relief swept through her body and she sobbed from the shock of her close brush with death.

'Are you OK?' he asked, pulling her head off his chest, his hands on either side of her face, his fingers buried in her hair.

'I thought I was never going to see Max again,' she cried, her face crumpling, and he pulled her head into his shoulder.

'I know,' he soothed, stroking her hair. 'I know.'

Sophie felt her fears recede as she wept and Daniel held her. Once again he had saved the day. Just as he had with Charlie and with Max. The horrifying events faded from her mind as she absorbed his calm strength and the sheer enormity of her love blossomed.

He held her while she cried and he kissed her hair, his own heart hammering. She was safe. She was safe. And he loved her. Not that it helped anything. In fact, it complicated everything, but it could not be ignored.

She moved in his arms and he felt her snuggle closer. How had he let this happen? And what was he going to do?

It was an impossible situation. As far as his head was concerned, she was still his brother's wife.

And, heaven help him, he loved her.

CHAPTER TEN

Max launched himself at his mother's sleeping form. 'Mummy, Mummy, Mummy,' he said, bouncing up and down beside her. 'Wake up. It's my birthday.'

Sophie opened her eyes slowly, the bright sunlight causing her to squint. 'Morning, baby,' she said, and accepted his sloppy kiss that missed her cheek and landed on her eye.

'You should see all my presents. It's so exciting, Mummy, come and see,' he said, dragging her up by her hand.

'All right, all right.' She laughed. 'Let me put my gown on. Anyone else up yet?'

'No. Just us,' he said.

'Lucky us.' She smiled. Max's blue eyes twinkled his excitement and she could feel herself respond to his childish wonder.

She flung on the red gown and tied the belt at her waist. She almost hadn't brought it but had changed her mind at the last minute. If Daniel wanted to be stoic then so be it, but she was damned if she'd make it easy for him.

'Better go and wake everyone up, sweetie,' she said and laughed as Max charged out of the room, yelling for everyone to get up because he wanted to open his presents.

Sophie shook her head. It was hard to believe it had only been two days ago that a maniac had held a knife to her throat. Life had quickly gone on as if nothing had happened, and she'd actually recovered quite quickly.

On this special day Sophie spared a thought for the poor soul who had held her for ransom. She had seen enough drug addicts come through St Jude's doors to know they had an illness. Once the immediate danger to her life had dissipated she had been able to look at the incident quite objectively.

The man had been caught within a few minutes. He hadn't stood a chance with four burly, fit security guards chasing him. Sophie marvelled at how he'd ever imagined he was going to pull it off.

But, she supposed, that was the tragedy of drugs. People did things they would never have done before they had got hooked, and how they scored their next hit didn't matter. As long as they scored.

Sophie actually felt sorry for the man in a lot of ways. What had happened in his life that had pushed him to addiction? Had he been an intelligent kid with promise or had he not stood much of a chance in life to begin with? What catalyst had driven him to the state of desperation he'd been in that night?

She shook her head—she would never know. She needed to stick to problems she could solve. Which brought her to Daniel. He was a different kind of addict. Addicted to his sense of obligation towards his brother born from his overriding guilt. She didn't know what to do about it either.

Sophie wandered into the lounge room where everyone was gathering around the central coffee-table laden with multicoloured gifts. Max was bouncing up and down on his haunches, impatient for the adults to join him. Sophie sat cross-legged on the floor and Max quickly jumped into her lap.

She could feel his little body trembling in anticipation and felt a pang of jealousy. Oh, to be a child and not have the worries of the world on your shoulders. As her mind buzzed with all her adult problems Max's simple life seemed very appealing.

Daniel sat on the lounge chair behind her. She didn't have to turn to confirm it, she could sense it. She didn't have to look either to know he would be wearing his boxer shorts and black snug-fitting T-shirt. And she didn't need eyes in the back of her head to feel his gaze boring straight through her.

Edward dished out the presents one at a time, as he did every year. The family watched as Max ripped the paper off each one, tearing through the pile of presents like a mini-tornado. He was disgustingly spoilt, as he was every year, but Sophie had given up protesting. He was a much-loved only grandchild, the littlest Monday, and though the family was generous they also expected him to be well mannered, polite and good.

'Here you are, Maxy,' said Daniel from behind, plonking a small wicker basket with a lid in front of them. It had a huge red bow tied around it and Sophie knew instantly what it was.

'Oh, wow, Unca Dan,' said Max, lifting the lid. 'A kitten, a kitten. Mummy, Unca Dan got me a kitten.' He lifted the tiny sleeping ball of fur gently out of the basket and brought it to his face, rubbing his cheek against the soft fur. 'How did you know, Unca Dan? How did you know?'

Everyone laughed. Max had wanted a kitten all year and hadn't exactly been keeping it a secret!

'Daniel!' she exclaimed, turning to look at him.

'He wanted a kitten.' He shrugged and grinned at his Max's totally enchanted expression.

'He's too young,' she protested.

'He'll be fine, I'll teach him how to care for her.'

Sophie shot him a dubious look. 'I think Daniel needs a big kiss for that, don't you?' she said to her son, and Daniel grinned, knowing he had won.

Max rose from her lap, taking his precious bundle with him, crawling up onto Daniel's lap and pressing a kiss on Daniel's cheek.

'This is the best present ever, Unca Dan. I love you.' Max snuggled into Daniel's embrace a little further, the sleeping kitten cradled between Max's little chest and Daniel's flat stomach. Father and son stared at the tiny animal, totally engrossed.

'I love you too, Maxy.'

Sophie turned away, blinking hard. A lump rose in her throat. She caught John's eye and felt a surge of guilt. She knew she should tell Daniel about his son, and in a lot of ways it would probably get her what she wanted. But she didn't want Daniel out of obligation. He was very good at obligation and he would want to do the right thing by her, but she was only interested if he loved her, wanted her.

If they were to ever get past everything, it would need to be because he loved her, not because he wanted to be a father to Max. She'd waited too long to settle for less.

The more she thought about it, the more it crystallised in her mind. She needed to get away. She couldn't live with

Daniel and this thing between them and stay sane. Finding somewhere new to live would become a priority when they returned to Brisbane.

The morning idled by. Sophie and Max walked down to the beach for a swim around nine before the sun got too hot. When they came back Sophie joined everyone in the kitchen and helped prepare the birthday lunch.

Daniel took Max out onto the deck and they played with the now awake and playful kitten. He talked to his young charge about cats and Max listened with rapt attention. Daniel's deep rumbling voice would occasionally be heard, followed by Max's higher giggle.

Sophie tried not to watch them as she helped with the meal preparations, but the bank of windows running the full length of the massive deck gave them spectacular ocean views and so the two figures on the deck were a little hard to ignore.

Plus, every time she looked out through the windows she was reminded of exactly what she and Daniel had done against that glass, and she spent an inordinate amount of time blushing. Her body was swamped with images from that night and how she managed to not cut herself on the vegetable peeler was a miracle, given the trembling of her hands.

They ate at about one and Daniel brought Max in on his shoulders, the kitten held firmly in place on Daniel's head by a chubby little hand.

'Ah. Hands, both of you, and put the cat back in her basket, sweetie. No kittens at the table.'

'Come on, matey,' said Daniel, rolling his eyes at Max dramatically and being rewarded by a naughty giggle. 'Better do as Mummy says.'

They ate until they were all groaning, only just managing to fit in a slice of Max's birthday cake. Shortly after that Sophie put a sleepy Max to bed for his nap and sat and watched her blond-haired, blue-eyed boy for a while. The kitten, who had been named Clementine, lay curled up beside him and he looked so happy Sophie almost changed her mind about moving out.

Max would hate it. The family would hate it. She'd hate it. But it wasn't like she was going to drop out of the Mondays' lives altogether. She just needed a breather from the constant ache inside that seemed to magnify every time she ran into Daniel. It would still be there, she knew that, but hopefully it would plateau instead of constantly peaking to new highs.

Sophie heard the front doorbell chime as she shut Max's door, and heard Daniel answer it. Edward, Wendy, John, Sally and Charlie were out on the deck and Sophie thought about joining them, but the comfy double lounge beckoned and she lay on it, thinking that a small nap was in order.

'Anthony!' said Daniel, surprised to see the family lawyer standing on their doorstep. 'What brings you here? Come in.'

'Ah, no, thanks, Daniel. I'm on my way to my wife's family for dinner I just had to drop this in.'

The elderly lawyer, not that much younger than John, handed Daniel a yellow envelope with something that felt like a videotape inside. It was addressed to him and to Sophie—or rather Mrs Michael Monday.

Daniel ran his fingers over her name. It sure put things into perspective. She was Mrs Michael Monday and he would do well to keep reminding himself of that. 'What is it?' he asked.

'It's a videotape that Michael made for both of you just before he and Sophie got married. He asked me to keep it safe and in the event of his death deliver it to you on Max's birthday two years after the date of his demise.'

Daniel felt his heart start to thud a little harder in his chest. What was on the tape?

'OK? If that's it, I'll be going,' said Anthony, interrupting Daniel's swirling thoughts. He mopped the sweat off his brow, the hot sun beaming down on his bald head.

'Of course,' said Daniel. 'Thank you for coming all this way, Anthony.' He shook the lawyer's hand before closing the door.

Michael, what have you done? He was tempted to go and watch it himself first but as it was addressed to both of them he knew that wasn't his right. Still, his hand trembled in anticipation.

'Sophie.'

'Hmm?' She didn't open her eyes. She didn't need the sight of Daniel in his boardies unsettling her equilibrium.

'This just arrived for us.'

She sighed sleepily and opened her eyes. 'What is it?'

'A videotape that Michael made. For you. And me.'

Sophie sat up and looked at the yellow envelope. She looked at Daniel and he seemed to be just as puzzled.

'What do we do with it?' she asked, afraid and nervous and apprehensive.

'Watch it, I guess,' he said quietly.

They went into the den and shut the door. Sophie watched as Daniel loaded the tape into the machine and pressed the play button. Neither of them sat down, but stood and waited for the tape to begin.

There was a minute of 'snow' and then Michael appeared on the screen, looking fit and alive. Sophie could feel herself choking up. She sat down on the chair behind her. It was too cruel for life to have taken Michael from them.

'Well, I guess if you're watching this I'm dead and have been for a couple of years. Poor me.' Michael laughed but it didn't really reach his eyes and she could tell that this video hadn't been easy for him to make.

'I guess you're wondering why I'm making this video. Well, tomorrow I'm marrying the girl I love. The girl I've loved since we were five and we played catch and kiss in the backyard.'

Sophie felt a tear spill down her cheek and she pulled a tissue out of the box that sat on the coffee-table in front of her.

'Sophie, I know you're going to make me the happiest man in the world. I'd like to thank you now for the time you gave me and for the son you bore me. He's not here yet but I want you to know that you've given me the greatest gift. One that, thanks to this wheelchair, I won't ever get a chance at again.'

Daniel could hear Sophie sniffling behind him and couldn't bear to look.

'But I'm doing this because I owe you an apology—owe you both an apology, actually. I know that you love me, Soph, as a best friend, a brother even, but not as a lover or a husband…and that's fine. I know you're in love with Daniel, have always been in love with Daniel, and I'm sorry that I've used our friendship and my…condition to get you to marry me. I should have encouraged you to patch things up with Daniel instead of seeing it as a way of having you for myself. I can only hope and pray that our marriage will be as happy for you as I know it's going to be for me. I'm going to make it my mission, Soph, to make you the happiest woman on earth.'

The tears were flowing freely down her face now. It had been. No, it hadn't been a marriage in the truest sense of the word, but she'd been very happy married to Michael.

'I guess I owe the biggest apology to you, Daniel. It doesn't matter how many times I tell you that it wasn't your fault and I don't blame you, I can still feel your guilt. You said to me not long ago that there must be some part of me that blames you, and you know what? I think you're right. I think there is a small part of me that's pissed at you about the accident. Not because I think it was your fault but because you walked away without a scratch and I'm crippled.'

Daniel felt his breath being torn out of his lungs and he reached back and sat in the chair next to Sophie. To hear Michael talk about this was cathartic. He'd always known that his brother had to have held some grudge, and to hear it finally was a relief.

'And I think it's that part that's been able to rationalise the terrible thing I've done to both of you. You see, Daniel, I knew Sophie was pregnant that day I intimated to you that she and I had also been fooling around.'

Sophie gasped at Michael's admission. He had told Daniel that he and her…that they'd… What on earth for? Why would he do such a thing?

'She visited me that morning and broke down about being pregnant and how worried she was about what you would say because you'd hardly been speaking since the accident and what bad timing it was. And I told her that you'd be a fool not to sweep her up in your arms and that if you didn't, I'd marry her. And that got me thinking that day about the possibility, and how marrying Sophie would make life in a wheelchair bearable. Because I loved her and always had, but I knew that, while she loved me, she was *in* love with you and I would never stand a chance. So that's when I decided to meddle.'

Daniel couldn't believe what he was hearing. All the things he had believed over the last couple of years were being shattered. He looked at Sophie and she looked back at him equally bewildered.

'That part of me that was pissed at you decided that you owed me. Now, that's not rational or fair, I know that, but I was a little desperate a couple of months ago. I knew that day that I'd be seeing you before she would and so I told you that the only thing that would make me want to go on with my life would be to marry Sophie. I led you to believe we were having a sexual relationship when we weren't, and I told you that if you really wanted me to be happy you'd let Sophie go and suggest she marry me instead. I knew your guilt ran deep and I played on it. And you did the rest. Much better than I could have planned. You dumped her that night before she had a chance to tell you about the baby, and she came straight to me.'

Sophie sat shell-shocked, listening to Michael's admissions. Daniel had given her to Michael because his brother had emotionally blackmailed him into it. Not because he hadn't loved her but because his brother had orchestrated it. Michael had played with their lives. Sophie felt anger mix with her disbelief.

'Am I proud of what I've done? No. I can only say in

my defence that two months ago I wasn't sure if I even wanted to live, and the only thing that dragged me out of the terrible, terrible darkness was the thought of forming a family with you and the baby, Sophie.'

She felt her anger soften. He was right. What a totally screwed-up time it had been for all of them emotionally. There had been anger and sadness, blame, guilt and desperation. Michael's depression had worried the entire family and they had all been grateful, not least her, when their engagement had given him a new lease of life.

It would be easy to judge Michael harshly now, his four-year-old actions removed from the dreadful roller-coaster of feelings they had all suffered. What a terrible time it had been. None of them had been thinking very rationally.

'So, I guess you're wondering why I've decided to make this tape? Easy. Guilt. I guess that's something we all know a lot about. I'd like to think that, as I'm obviously not around any more, you two will have found a way to come together. But if I know Daniel as well as I think I do then he's probably still in New York, nursing his guilt, trying to keep away from you, Sophie. I figured you two might need a little nudge.

'So why now? Why did I instruct Anthony to deliver it to you now? I thought two years seemed like a reasonable amount of time to have elapsed. I figured any sooner and society might not have thought it proper for you two to get together. I just hope I'm not too late. If you're both sitting here, watching this, and have already worked it out or are married to different people then I guess I'm going to look like a right idiot.

'I'm just really sorry to have meddled in your lives and

interrupted a great love match. I expect you'll both be pretty mad at me by now. I only hope you can forgive me in time and realise that we were all victims of circumstance to a degree.

'Daniel, let it go, man. This isn't your fault and you've paid the price too long. If you really feel like you need to make atonement, I think you have more than done that, don't you? Love her, man. Love her like she deserves to be loved.

'Sophie, remember me to our son. I love you and I'm sorry. I love you both and I hope you both live happily ever after.'

The screen went blank and they both sat staring at it. Neither of them moved for a while and then Daniel got up and walked over to the window, watching the gulls ride the air currents.

'So…I'm Max's father.'

'Yes,' said Sophie quietly.

There was silence again. Where did they even begin? There was so much to say, to talk about.

'Did you really believe that I was having sex with Michael at the same time we were lovers? How could you have thought that of me?'

'Honestly? Deep down I didn't. It seems like this is the day for honesty so I think I can finally admit it to myself. I think a part of me knew that Michael was lying and I just suppressed it, ignored it. He was asking me for you and it was easier to do it when I could pretend that you were unfaithful.'

'Your guilt really ran that deep? That you would give me up like I was some kind of prize?' Outrage at the disregard of both Michael and Daniel for her as a person, a human being, took over. They had traded her like some bartering chip. Your lover for your guilt!

'My brother couldn't walk because of me, Soph. That was a terrible burden. I know I had no right to use you to assuage my guilt but I just wanted to make it right for him.'

'Damn right. You had no right.'

'Hey, it wasn't my idea and anyway…it didn't help.'

Sophie sighed and walked over to where he stood. He was right. Michael had definitely been pulling their strings. 'And what about now? Does the tape help?'

'Yes, it does, actually. It was freaky to see him again, so alive. A bit like a ghost. But I do feel absolved. Michael being pissed at me I can handle. We were brothers. But I took that as blame and I didn't need his when I had so much of my own.'

'So if part of you knew I hadn't been unfaithful then you must have known Max was yours.'

'I guess…yes,' he said. 'But I didn't know you were pregnant until I was in New York and I knew what being a father meant to Michael. He'd told me the accident had left him impotent, and it was just another thing to feel guilty about, so when he had this chance I couldn't deny it. I blocked out the little voice that kept whispering the truth. Again, it was easier to ignore the truth and believe what he wanted me to believe.'

Sophie nodded again. Michael had sure done a number on their heads. 'So when you told me that you didn't love me, that you had lied to get me into bed…that was a lie?'

'Of course it was,' he sighed. 'I would never have told you I loved you if I hadn't. But I needed to make sure that you sought solace in Michael's arms. I'm so sorry, it was harsh, but I needed to destroy the love you had for me to push you to Michael. I needed there to be no doubt whatsoever in your mind that you and I were over.'

'Well, it worked.'

'I'm so sorry,' he said, stroking his hand down her cheek. 'I've never stopped loving you. I fooled myself for a while. Moving away helped, but the other night, when that guy held a knife to your throat, it hit me. I still loved you.'

She nodded. His admission started her heart beating erratically. Still, caution was required. 'Seems like there's a *but* there.'

'No buts, Sophie. For the first time in four years I feel free. I feel free to tell you how I feel and to think we could have a life together. But I've behaved so badly since I've been back that I can't possibly expect you to feel the same way. I know I've hurt you a lot over the years. I can't blame you if you hate me and want nothing to do with me. I do want to be involved with Max but I'll be guided by you. I won't push.'

'Daniel, you idiot.' She laughed, hardly believing what she was hearing. 'I love you. Yes, between you and your brother I've been hurt and I thought, like you, that I was over this, but when we made love the other night I knew I'd never stopped loving you. I want us to be together and for Max to know you as his father. We've spent too many years apart, lets not waste any more time.'

Daniel stood still. There was only a small gap separating them but he was too stunned to close it. He blinked hard and opened his eyes again and she was still there with that silly grin on her face and that look of expectancy. Had she really said those words? Did she really mean them? Surely this was too good to be true.

'Really? You want us to be a family?'

'Really, you silly man. I love you, Danny. I've always loved you. From the moment you called me brat when I was five and you were eleven, I was a goner.'

Sophie couldn't believe that he still hadn't moved to close the gap between them. She wanted to feel his lips against hers so badly she could practically taste him.

'Danny! If you don't kiss me in the next second I'm going to think this is all a cruel joke.'

Sophie wasn't sure if he kissed her or she kissed him in the end. All she knew was that she was in the arms of the man she loved and that finally everything was right with the world.

'How are we going to tell the family?' she asked some time later as she sat cuddled in his arms in the lounge chair.

'I guess we'll just show them the tape,' Daniel said.

Max chose that moment to barge into the room and spied his mother and uncle curled up together on the couch.

'There you are, Mummy,' he said, and plonked himself and Clementine between them. He squirmed a bit, making himself a nice comfy spot, and relaxed against Daniel's chest.

'Why are you hugging my mummy, Unca Dan?' asked Max.

'Um…ah..' Daniel shrugged at Sophie, lost for words.

'Do you love Mummy?'

'Ah…yes, I do, actually, Max. Is that OK?'

'Sure. Are you gonna marry her?'

'As long as it's OK by you,' said Daniel, shooting a withering look at Sophie who was trying hard not to laugh.

'Does that mean you'll be my daddy?'

'I guess it does.'

'Will I have to call you Daddy or can I keep calling you Unca Dan?'

'Whatever you want, Maxy,' said Daniel, holding his breath for his son's next decree.

'I think I'll call you Daddy.'

'Okey-dokey,' said Daniel, wanting to shout his joy from the rooftops. He ruffled Max's hair instead, not wanting to frighten his son with the strength of his feelings.

'That OK, Mummy?' asked Max.

'Sure,' said Sophie, all choked up. She was thankful that Max was too engrossed in Clementine to pay any heed to the tears that were falling down her face.

Daniel kissed her forehead and she was surprised to see moisture shimmering in his blue eyes.

'I love you,' she mouthed over the top of Max's head, and he mouthed it back.

The trio sat cuddling contentedly on the lounge, being the family they should have been before life had got in the way. Sophie stroked Max's hair and reflected on the irony of the situation. The person who had kept them apart was the same person who had brought them back together. And now, thanks to Michael, they were finally free to love each other for ever.

NEEDED: FULL-TIME FATHER
by Carol Marinelli

The grand opening of Heatherton A&E doesn't quite go to plan, so nurse manager Madison Walsh must rely on, and trust, new consultant Guy Boyd to save the day. Trusting turns to loving, but Madison has her daughter's happiness to consider...

TELL ME YOU LOVE ME *by Gill Sanderson*

John Cameron is a loner, travelling the world as a professional diver. For reasons of his own he's wary of getting close to anyone – until he meets Dr Abbey Fraser. John instinctively knows he needs to be part of her life. Then they discover they share a secret...

THE SURGEON'S ENGAGEMENT WISH
by Alison Roberts

Nurse Beth Dawson has chosen small town life for some peace and quiet. The last person she expects to meet is Luke Savage, the high-flying surgeon she was once engaged to! Luke has changed, mellowed – realised what's important in life. But will he forgive Beth for leaving him?

A&E DRAMA: Pulses are racing in these
fast-paced dramatic stories

On sale 3rd February 2006

4 FREE

BOOKS AND A SURPRISE GIFT!

We would like to take this opportunity to thank you for reading this Mills & Boon® book by offering you the chance to take FOUR more specially selected titles from the Medical Romance™ series absolutely FREE! We're also making this offer to introduce you to the benefits of the Reader Service™—

- ★ FREE home delivery
- ★ FREE gifts and competitions
- ★ FREE monthly Newsletter
- ★ Exclusive Reader Service offers
- ★ Books available before they're in the shops

Accepting these FREE books and gift places you under no obligation to buy, you may cancel at any time, even after receiving your free shipment. Simply complete your details below and return the entire page to the address below. You don't even need a stamp!

YES! Please send me 4 free Medical Romance books and a surprise gift. I understand that unless you hear from me, I will receive 6 superb new titles every month for just £2.75 each, postage and packing free. I am under no obligation to purchase any books and may cancel my subscription at any time. The free books and gift will be mine to keep in any case.

M6ZED

Ms/Mrs/Miss/Mr ....Initials ....

BLOCK CAPITALS PLEASE

Surname ....

Address ....

....

....Postcode...

Send this whole page to:
UK: FREEPOST CN81, Croydon, CR9 3WZ

Offer valid in UK only and is not available to current Reader service subscribers to this series. Overseas and Eire please write for details. We reserve the right to refuse an application and applicants must be aged 18 years or over. Only one application per household. Terms and prices subject to change without notice. Offer expires 30th April 2006. As a result of this application, you may receive offers from Harlequin Mills & Boon and other carefully selected companies. If you would prefer not to share in this opportunity please write to The Data Manager, PO Box 676, Richmond, TW9 1WU.

Mills & Boon® is a registered trademark owned by Harlequin Mills & Boon Limited.
Medical Romance™ is being used as a trademark. The Reader Service™ is being used as a trademark.